What Disappears in Vegas . . .

Read all the mysteries in the
NANCY DREW DIARIES

Nancy Drew

DIARIES™

What Disappears in Vegas . . .

#25

CAROLYN KEENE

Aladdin

NEW YORK LONDON TORONTO SYDNEY NEW DELHI

ALADDIN

An imprint of Simon & Schuster Children's Publishing Division

1230 Avenue of the Americas, New York, New York 10020

First Aladdin paperback edition January 2024

Text copyright © 2024 by Simon & Schuster, LLC.

Cover illustration copyright © 2024 by Erin McGuire

Also available in an Aladdin hardcover edition.

All rights reserved, including the right of reproduction in whole or in part in any form.

ALADDIN and related logo are registered trademarks of Simon & Schuster, LLC.

NANCY DREW, NANCY DREW DIARIES, and colophons are registered trademarks of Simon & Schuster, LLC.

Simon & Schuster: Celebrating 100 Years of Publishing in 2024

For information about special discounts for bulk purchases, please contact Simon & Schuster Special Sales at 1-866-506-1949 or business@simonandschuster.com.

The Simon & Schuster Speakers Bureau can bring authors to your live event. For more information or to book an event contact the Simon & Schuster Speakers Bureau at 1-866-248-3049 or visit our website at www.simonspeakers.com.

Series designed by Karin Paprocki

Cover designed by Alicia Mikles

Interior designed by Mike Rosamilia

The text of this book was set in Adobe Caslon Pro.

Manufactured in the United States of America 1223 OFF

2 4 6 8 10 9 7 5 3 1

Library of Congress Cataloging-in-Publication Data

Names: Keene, Carolyn, author.

Title: What disappears in Vegas ... / Carolyn Keene.

Description: First Aladdin paperback edition. | New York : Aladdin, 2024. | Series: Nancy Drew diaries ; #25 | Audience: Ages 8 to 12. | Summary: Nancy investigates the disappearance of the bride while attending the wedding of her friends Bess and George's cousin Veronica's wedding to the owner of local extreme sports complex in Las Vegas.

Identifiers: LCCN 2023042823 (print) | LCCN 2023042824 (ebook) | ISBN 9781665939461 (hardcover) | ISBN 9781665939454 (paperback) | ISBN 9781665939478 (ebook)

Subjects: CYAC: Missing persons—Fiction. | Weddings—Fiction. | Extreme sports—Fiction. | Las Vegas (Nev.)—Fiction. | Mystery and detective stories. | LCGFT: Detective and mystery fiction. | Novels.

Classification: LCC PZ7.K23 Wh 2024 (print) | LCC PZ7.K23 (ebook) | DDC [Fic]—dc23

LC record available at https://lccn.loc.gov/2023042823

LC ebook record available at https://lccn.loc.gov/2023042824

Contents

What Disappears in Vegas . . .

Dear Diary,

I THINK I'M MORE OF A REALIST THAN a romantic, but let's face it: weddings can be a lot of fun. Which is why I'm super excited to be invited to tag along to Bess and George's cousin Veronica's wedding. It's taking place in Las Vegas! On top of a huge skyscraper! And crazier still, Veronica and her fiancé, Xavier, are going to BASE jump off the roof deck when the ceremony is over. Xavier owns the Redd Zone, a big extreme-sports complex in town.

I just hope everything goes according to plan. Don't tell anyone, but I'm not exactly an extreme-sports fan, and I hope there's no pressure to do anything dangerous. I mean, I like excitement as much as anyone! But I want everyone to survive the wedding. . . .

CHAPTER ONE

Extreme Engagement

"OMIGOSH, NANCY," MY FRIEND BESS SAID, peering over the guardrail of a pedestrian bridge. It was a long drop: roughly fifteen stories down a rocky fissure to a rushing river. "Remind me why I agreed to this."

I turned and shared a significant look with George, Bess's cousin and my other good friend. *I* couldn't imagine why Bess had decided to bungee jump off this bridge, and I was guessing that George couldn't either. Bungee jumping off this bridge was something that might appear in one of my nightmares. I like my feet firmly planted on the ground, thanks. But Bess has always been a little different: she likes to drive fast, take risks, and ride every roller coaster in a hundred-mile radius. Plus, we were at a barbecue thrown by Bess and George's cousin Veronica, and Veronica's boyfriend owned the largest extreme-sports complex in Chicago: Redd Zone. As a surprise to the guests, Xavier had his team set up a bungee jump just steps away from the park where we'd been enjoying our hot dogs and hamburgers. All of us guests were welcome to try it—after signing a huge stack of waivers and legal documents.

Bess had already signed on the dotted lines and was all suited up.

"Well, better you than me," George said, and I swatted her on the arm.

"George! I think Bess is looking for *comfort*."

Bess's eyes cut from George (irritated) to me (grateful). "This is fine, isn't it, Nancy?" she asked hopefully, shifting in the heavy safety gear. "I mean, I'll be fine. Everything will be . . ."

"Everything's going to be *fantastic*." Xavier suddenly stepped up behind Bess, tugging on her harness, tightening a few places, and then smiling. He had short, dark hair, deep-set brown eyes, and a million-dollar smile. His face adorned all the Redd Zone's advertising, and Veronica had told us that he was super active on social media. He'd been filming the barbecue and the bungee jumps on and off, promising that we'd see them on Redd Zone's social media—if we didn't mind "being famous."

"This is the best decision you ever made," he went on, looking Bess right in the eye. "Look at this scenery! It's going to be amazing. This is why I got into this business: this is going to make you feel *so alive*."

When he nodded at Bess, I could see some of the tension leave her body. "I want that," she said, nodding back at him. "I definitely want to feel *alive!*"

George nudged me. *As opposed to . . . ?* she mouthed. I smirked but shook my head. I was with George: just breathing was enough for me to feel alive. But then, I wasn't Redd Zone's target customer.

"This has to be really expensive," George whispered so only I could hear. She gestured around at the bridge, the equipment, the waiver forms. "Bungee jumping is pricey because of all the equipment and the insurance you have to have. And they're letting all the guests do it?"

I nodded. "I guess Redd Zone is doing well," I whispered back. Maybe a lot of people in Chicago wanted to feel "*alive.*"

Bess was only the third person to bungee jump. Everyone crowded around to watch as Xavier encouraged her to step up on a small flight of stairs that put her level with the guardrail, onto a rubber mat. Bess stepped up, a little shakily, and I could see her taking a deep breath.

"You've got this, Bess!" I yelled, then let out a little whoop. Other people in the crowd started cheering too.

"You're going to kill it, *prima*!" Veronica's sister, Deanna, yelled.

"Yeah!" Veronica stepped up beside her. "Kicking butt runs in the family!"

A few relatives whooped and clapped. George chuckled.

On top of the steps, Bess seemed to relax a little bit. She shook out her arms and let out a huff, nodding as she looked back at the crowd and smiled.

"Go show that river who's boss, cuz!" George shouted.

Bess looked at her and laughed, then glanced at Xavier. His brother, Max, his partner in the Redd Zone, had stepped up and started checking all the safety equipment. He gave the thumbs-up to Xavier, who turned to Bess with a grin and nodded.

"Shall we count down?" he asked. When Bess said okay, he began, "Ten . . . nine . . . eight . . . seven . . ."

The crowd joined in. "Six . . . five . . ."

When we got to "three," Bess jumped. George and I let out little gasps of surprise, and the crowd whooped appreciatively. Bess did always like to defy expectations.

George and I leaned over to watch her fall.

"Yiiiiiiiiiiiiiiiiikes!" she screamed as she plummeted down toward the water.

My heart was in my throat just watching. *Okay, stop now, reach the end of the cord, start bouncing. . . .* I'd seen it happen for the other two jumpers, but still, it was terrifying to watch my friend free-fall down this rocky gorge. There was no way she would survive that fall. There was no way anyone could. . . .

"Ahhhhhh—Oh!" Bess's scream cut off as she was startled by being jerked back up. She'd finally reached the end of the bungee cord, just yards from the river. Now she began bouncing up and down, laughing hysterically.

"That was *amazing*!" she shouted.

Relief flooded my body. "You did it, Bess!" I yelled.

"You survived!" George added.

But Bess was laughing too hard to respond. "That was the best thing I've ever dooooooone!" she shouted after a few seconds.

"I told you!" Xavier yelled back.

As Bess continued to laugh and whoop, and

Xavier and Max worked on hauling her back up, I stepped away from the guardrail and ran my hand through my hair. I had that weird numb feeling I got sometimes after a stressful standoff, or a near miss with a bad guy. Nothing had happened, I knew, and Bess had always been safe. Still, I felt like I needed a minute to walk it off.

I felt a hand on my arm and turned to see George. She gave me a gentle squeeze. "So she's okay," she said quietly. Her dark eyes were warm with relief.

I nodded. "She's okay," I repeated, putting my hand over hers and squeezing back. I knew we were feeling the same way.

Sometimes it's hard, loving a daredevil.

We headed back to the park to celebrate Bess's survival with guava and cheese empanadas. "Mmmmm," Bess moaned, flicking a bit of guava paste from her cheek into her mouth, "I *love* Auntie Elena's empanadas. Mine never come out as good, even when I make her recipes."

George grinned. "My dad says Uncle Rick won the lottery when he married Elena, because he can't even boil rice," she said.

Bess chuckled. "He makes up for it in other ways," she said. "Remember, he drove Veronica and Deanna to all their soccer and swim meets."

As we ate, a bunch of other guests stepped up to make the jump. Bess had the flushed, giddy look of someone who just passed her driving test for the first time, or aced her last final exam. As for me, I focused on my pie and stopped watching the jumpers. I was glad Bess had had fun, but this wasn't for me.

"It was amazing," Bess told us between bites. "I could feel, like, the adrenaline rushing through my body and then when I stopped, it was this massive relief. And suddenly I felt like all my senses were on overdrive, you know? I could see more clearly, I could hear you guys talking up above and my own heartbeat. I swear I could *smell* the plants in the river and the flowers on the shore. I just felt, like, super *alive*."

"It sounds great," I said honestly. "But I'm not sure

extreme sports will ever be my thing. I like feeling alive right here, with my two feet on the ground, not falling or hurtling in any one direction."

Bess chuckled.

"You're a pragmatist, Nancy," George said with a smile. "And I think I'm the same. In real life, anyway. I like to take my risks behind the safety of a computer screen."

We ate and chatted a little more. Bess and George's cousin Deanna came over with her three-year-old daughter, Miranda, and soon we were all asking her questions, giggling at her funny responses, and watching her observe the bungee jumping.

"Do *you* want to jump?" George asked her with a big smile.

Miranda looked at her as though she'd asked whether Miranda wanted to fly to the moon. "I'm too little!"

Bess chuckled. "But if you *were* old enough, would you want to do it? Be a risk-taker like your big cousin Bess?"

Miranda gave Bess a hard look with her wide brown eyes, her guava-stained lower lip pushed out in concentration.

"No," she said finally. "I think that's silly. But Tía Veronica is doing it."

She pointed toward the bridge, and we all turned to look. Sure enough, Veronica seemed to be getting suited up—along with Xavier.

"Are they jumping *together*?" George asked with a smirk. "How romantic!"

Bess nudged her with her elbow. "The couple that plummets together, summits together."

George and I both groaned and rolled our eyes. "You had to work for that one," George remarked.

"It was a stretch," Deanna agreed with a chuckle.

Bess widened her eyes in mock hurt. "Really, you guys? I thought it was pretty—"

"Hey, everyone!"

Max's voice rose over the crowd, and we could see him walking toward the park and gesturing for everyone to come back to the bridge. "Our hosts are about to make a tandem jump, and they would love your support! Come on over to the bridge and try to act as excited as you were the first time!"

Deanna, George, Bess, and I all exchanged glances, then got to our feet, Deanna swinging Miranda onto her hip.

"Let's go see Tía Veronica make this silly jump, huh?" she said, squeezing Miranda close.

Soon we were all assembled back on the bridge. It was crowded enough to make me a little nervous, so I packed myself in tight next to Bess and George and secretly hung on to a railing behind us. Fifteen stories is a lot!

All suited up now, Xavier turned to address the crowd as Veronica wound her long, dark hair into a knot at the top of her head and secured it with an elastic. "Thank you so much for coming," he said, taking in the crowd with his warm brown eyes. "You guys all mean so much to us, family and friends, some old, some new. We love all of you and really wanted you to all be here to witness . . . this." He waved behind him, at Veronica and the guardrail where they were about to jump from. But then, suddenly, Xavier swiveled around and crouched down, landing on one knee. As he reached into his sweatshirt pocket and brought out a small box, Veronica brought both hands up to her face and shrieked.

"What are you doing!" she cried, shaking her head. "You aren't . . . omigosh!"

Xavier just beamed at her. "Veronica," he said, "*mi amor*. I love you more than anything, and I want to create a future with you, a family with you, *so many* more adventures with you!"

He flipped open the box, revealing a brilliant square diamond set in a simple gold band. As Veronica gasped, Xavier chuckled. "Don't worry, *mi amor*, it's lab grown. Only the most ethical jewelry for my love!"

Veronica shook her head, and Xavier went on. "*Amor*, will you take the jump with me and be my wife?" He looked up hopefully, and Veronica took her hands away from her face and smiled.

"Xavier—my rock! I . . ."

Xavier suddenly jumped to his feet and gestured for her to stop. "Wait!" he said, taking her hand and leading her up the steps to the guardrail. "Tell me on the way down! I want this to be a moment we never forget."

Veronica laughed, glancing back at the crowd. "Okay. Only you, Xavier! I knew if you ever proposed, it would be unique, but . . ."

Xavier squeezed her hand. Max stepped up and quickly checked all the safety restraints, then gave the thumbs-up. Xavier encouraged us all to count down.

"Ten . . . nine . . . eight . . ."

At "one," they jumped, still holding hands. We heard Veronica scream as they fell, and Xavier's excited whoop. Finally, they hit the end of the cord and bounced back, and both began laughing and whooping hysterically.

"She said *yes*!" Xavier yelled as they bounced up and down. All of us on the bridge began clapping and cheering as Xavier added, "Hope you're all ready for the most thrilling wedding *of all time* . . . because you're all invited!"

CHAPTER TWO

Sin City

"WOW, BESS—IS THERE ANYTHING YOU *didn't* bring?"

Bess glanced at her cousin and shrugged, pushing her giant hard-sided suitcase ahead of us in the line to check in for our flight. It was a month after the barbecue, and we were headed to Veronica and Xavier's wedding in Las Vegas. The airport was a madhouse, but thankfully Ned dropped us off two hours before our flight was scheduled to depart. He's good like that. We'd just said our goodbyes, and although we'd only be gone for a few days, I already missed him.

"Well, George," Bess said, "I wanted to be prepared. Veronica made it clear that in addition to the wedding, there would be arrival cocktails, a rehearsal dinner, a brunch after the wedding . . . I need a separate outfit for each! Unlike you, I won't wear the same black dress to *everything*."

George huffed in mock offense and rolled her eyes. "It's a classic for a reason, cuz."

Bess pushed her suitcase ahead as the line moved forward, twisting it sideways as we reached a bend, and looked back at me. "Nancy brought a pretty big suitcase too," she said. "Nance, aren't you excited? I love weddings! And this one's in *Vegas*!"

"Oh, sure." I smiled, though if I was being honest, I was feeling a little trepidatious about this *particular* wedding. It was super kind of Veronica and Xavier to include me, even if George and I had agreed to babysit the little kids during the ceremony so their parents could focus on the happy couple. Bess was going to be one of Veronica's bridesmaids. But they'd also made it clear from the very beginning that this was going to be an unusual wedding—an *extreme* wedding, with lots of extreme sports mixed into the traditional activities. The itinerary they'd sent out with the invitations included several get-togethers, but few details about what crazy stunts were planned—or when. Or performed by *who*. I knew the ceremony would take place on the roof-deck of the Soar, the casino hotel where we'd be staying, which was shaped like an ice pick, over fifty stories tall, that jutted into the sky. The roof-deck had an outcropping with a glass floor where you could feel like you were floating over the Strip, and a roller coaster that wound around the outside of the top few stories. Veronica and Xavier planned to ride the roller coaster, get married, and then celebrate with a BASE jump off the casino roof-deck.

Honestly, it made my palms sweaty just thinking about it.

"It's too bad Uncle Russ had to work," Bess was saying.

George shrugged. "Yeah, and it's a shame your parents already agreed to go to that graduation party. But

I guess that's the risk of planning a wedding quickly."

Bess nodded. "And honestly? I'm kind of psyched to be heading to Vegas, just the three of us," she said. "I mean, I'm not planning to get into any kind of '*what happens in Vegas stays in Vegas*' trouble. But I think we'll have a lot of fun, just us girls."

I smiled and nodded, though I still had a pit in my stomach. I was hoping I could survive this whole weekend by smiling and nodding and clapping enthusiastically for those who *chose* to take part in the extreme activities. But Xavier seemed so gung ho, and he was clear on the invitation that he would be filming all the events and posting them on social media to promote the Redd Zone. I just hoped I could sit out politely without looking like a party pooper.

I chatted with Bess about the outfits I'd packed until we got up to the desk to check in. Bess fancies herself a "flying expert," so George and I hung back and smiled serenely while Bess used all her charm to try to get us the best seats possible on our bargain-basement fares. To my amazement, she'd soon secured us the exit row with extra legroom. We thanked the clerk effusively and headed off to security.

A couple of hours later, we were settling into our exit-row seats when someone squeezed George's shoulder on the way down the aisle. "Hey, cuz! I guess we're on the same flight!"

We all looked up to find Deanna, holding Miranda and guiding her older son down the aisle. Her husband, Eduardo, was placing their bags in the overhead compartment a few rows back.

"Hey, Deanna!" George said, and Bess and I said our hellos too.

Deanna got all set up with her family, and for the first hour or so of the flight, the three of us busied ourselves watching movies on the in-flight entertainment system (a Marvel movie for me, *Sleepless in Seattle* for Bess, and a documentary about Y2K for George). As we were all starting to get a little restless, Deanna suddenly popped up and settled herself in an empty seat across the aisle.

"How's it going, ladies?" she asked, ripping open a

bag of chips and taking a couple before offering them to us.

"Not so bad," George said, taking a couple of chips. "Did you know they seriously thought the world was going to *shut down* when the millennium turned, all because of some shortsighted programming?"

Deanna rolled her eyes. "Sounds fascinating, kiddo. But right now I'm just hoping this plane's computers are programmed right."

"Are you afraid to fly?" Bess asked. "How come I didn't know that about you?"

Deanna shrugged and crunched a chip. "I'm not like, *afraid* afraid. I'd just rather not fly, if I have a choice." She swallowed. "Anyway, I guess my sister's wedding is a good enough reason to take the risk. God knows she'll be taking enough this weekend."

George grinned. "Which is the bigger risk?" she asked. "Jumping off a fifty-story casino, or getting married?"

"Ha!" Deanna snorted. "Look, my kids wear me out, but married life is working for me. And I don't think Veronica has anything to worry about, marrying Xavier. That dude *adores* her."

Bess raised an eyebrow. "What about your parents? I remember Veronica told me that at first, Aunt Elena and Uncle Rick were *not* huge fans of his."

"Oh well." Deanna sighed. "They're still not, honestly. Like, they're not coming to the wedding."

George sat up in her seat. "Really? Why not?"

"They said this was all too rushed. From engagement to vows in a month? '*Why not wait a year and see if you still feel the same?*' they asked Veronica. But honestly, I think he just rubs them the wrong way," Deanna said, shaking her head. "He's a big personality, I know that. And Veronica's always been more quiet. My mom thinks Xavier steamrolls over her, gets her to do whatever he wants. Like her whole interest in extreme sports now—Mom thinks he's pushing that on her. But I think that's only because they've never seen her *do* it, you know? I've watched Veronica bungee jumping and whatever. It's not just Xavier pushing her—she's genuinely having a great time."

Bess nodded. "It looks that way to me," she agreed.

"Though it is surprising," George added. "I mean, I agree with Deanna, Veronica seems like she's really having fun with this stuff. I just never would have expected it of her. I guess it just shows, you never know what will click with people."

Deanna crunched another chip, nodding thoughtfully. "I guess I'm biased," she said. "Eduardo and I introduced them, did you know that? He knows Xavier from high school." She offered the bag to us again and, when George waved it away, rolled down the top. "I think Xavier is a stand-up guy, and he brings out the best in Veronica. But you can't convince everybody." She shrugged again.

"It's too bad for Veronica," Bess said. "I'm sure she'd love for Auntie and Uncle to be there."

"Of course," Deanna agreed. "But I hope they'll come around once they see how happy Veronica and Xavier are after the wedding. And they can watch it online, if Xavier has anything to say about it."

George frowned. "Do you think that has anything

to do with their opinion of him?" she asked. "All the promotion for his complex? He's always filming and posting on social media. I could see where they might get the impression that it's all for show, and that Veronica's not really as excited about it as she seems."

Deanna sighed again. "I'm sure it doesn't help," she admitted. "You know—Mom and Dad are not the right age to be super into social media. I think it all seems a little weird to them, to not only be doing these daredevil things but to also be constantly hyping them up. But I also think none of that would matter if they just *liked* Xavier more or thought he was the right match for Veronica."

"I hope they prove your parents wrong," Bess said. "No offense to your parents."

Deanna nodded. "No, of course. None taken. I'm right there with you."

A sudden shriek sounded from behind us—a shriek that sounded remarkably like Miranda. Deanna startled and peered down the aisle behind her, then got to her feet.

"That's my alarm," she said. "Looks like nap time is over. Anyway, nice talking to you girls. I'll see you in Sin City, I guess!"

"See you in Sin City," we called as she hustled back to her assigned seat.

Bess, George, and I looked at one another for a moment, silently digesting that conversation. I wasn't sure what to say. Veronica and Xavier had always seemed fairy-tale levels of happy to me, and it was a big surprise to hear that her parents didn't approve. It seemed to cast a pall over our fun, celebratory weekend in Vegas.

"Well," George said finally, "that's kind of a bummer."

Bess nodded and sighed, then picked up her headphones and reached out to unpause her movie. "No offense, guys," she said, "but it's back to Meg Ryan and Tom Hanks for me. At least in rom-coms, love always prevails!"

"This might be the best view I've ever had from a hotel room," I mused a few hours later, peering out our thirty-second-floor window at the glittering Las Vegas Strip. It was still light outside, but the casinos seemed to sparkle in the late afternoon sun. The Soar was situated at the northern end, and our window faced south, meaning we could look right down the Strip at all the most famous casinos: the Toucan, the Polynesian, the Hong Kong, the Nile, the luxurious Volterre, and so many more. Each was lit up by thousands of glittering lights, programmed to flash and change into patterns, some random, some timed to the music that seemed to blare from speakers all up and down the Strip. Some had huge fountains in front that threw up giant plumes of water, forming all kinds of shapes, in repeating patterns. The Toucan had a landscaped faux rainforest out front, and the Polynesian had a man-made tropical lagoon.

Bess sidled up beside me, dressed to the nines in a rose-gold cocktail dress, her golden hair curled and fluffed around her face. "Isn't it amazing?" she asked. "I can't stop staring. The whole Strip is such a feast for the eyes."

"It's like an amusement park for adults," George agreed, clasping a necklace around the collar of her trusty little black dress—this necklace was a modern plastic design with bright shapes in blue, yellow, and green. "Are we still going to walk to the welcome drinks, or Bess, are you actually thinking of wearing those ridiculous shoes?" She pointed to Bess's glittering golden sandals, each of which had a three-inch platform heel.

Bess pouted. "Umm, I have flats that fit into my purse, like every fashionista," she replied, pulling a folded-up pair from her bag and quickly sitting down to switch footwear. "Of course we can walk. I want to see all these places up close!"

A few minutes later we were headed south on the Strip. I tugged self-consciously at the shiny green blouse that Ned always said made my eyes look bluer. I'm not really a dress-up kind of girl—I prefer outfits you can make a hasty getaway in. But tonight felt like the right opportunity to be fancy. The three of us were alone in Vegas, and I was ready to see the town.

We passed the fountain at the Volterre and paused to watch the water perform an elegant ballet set to *Rhapsody in Blue*. Other tourists clustered around us, all of us oohing and aahing at the carefully choreographed performance.

"Have you been inside?" the woman to my right asked as the music died down. She was probably around my dad's age, with short hair dyed bright red.

"No," I said. "We haven't been anywhere yet. I mean, except the Soar. We just arrived today."

The woman nodded, looking me up and down, then glanced at Bess and George. "Classy girls like you, you'd be right at home there. They have the best buffet, and they really take care of you when you're playing the slots." She mimed throwing back a drink. "I'm Edna, by the way."

"Uh, thanks, Edna. Actually, I'm not much of a gambler," I admitted.

Edna frowned. "What are you doing in Vegas then?"

"We're here for a wedding," Bess said.

"Oh, how romantic," Edna said approvingly. "My son Frankie, he got married at the chapel where the officiant is Elvis. I mean, the first time."

"Our cousin is getting married on the roof-deck of the Soar," George explained. "Then she's, well, BASE jumping off."

Edna's eyes widened. "Well, how about that," she said, smiling. "Best of luck to them. Really, best of luck."

We smiled and thanked her, then moved along, gawking at all the buildings as we made our way to the Polynesian.

The Polynesian was about midway down the Strip, a huge, dark wood structure that I guess was supposed to look like a Polynesian temple, but it was so big, it actually looked like "Polynesian temple meets shopping mall." There were tiki carvings lining the walkway to the front door, and a massive, turquoise-blue swimming pool that filled the five hundred yards or so between the casino and the Strip itself. The pool was landscaped to look like a tropical lagoon, with beautiful tropical foliage dipping down toward the bright blue water. As we walked along, I noticed that there was actually a small white-sand beach to the right of the casino entrance, where a few parents and little kids dipped their toes.

"Wow!" Bess said, taking in the pool with a shake of her head. "They really go all out on these casinos, huh? I feel like I'm in Maui—I mean, except for the intense dry heat!"

"At least it's getting cooler as the sun goes down. But yeah, I wonder how they keep these tropical plants alive?" George pondered out loud. "It can't be cheap! I wonder what this place is like inside."

I gestured to a small, roped-off terrace just on the other side of the beach. It was decorated with fairy lights and aqua and orange balloons—Veronica and Xavier's wedding colors. "Looks like we won't find out," I said. "The party seems to be outside."

We made our way over and greeted the guests who'd already arrived. Deanna was there, along with her husband and kids. She introduced us to Priya Laghari, the other bridesmaid and Veronica's best friend "since forever," as she put it. Priya had warm brown eyes and shiny black hair swept back in a low bun. She introduced us to her husband, Sumit, and their five-year-old daughter, Lakshmi.

"Where did you travel from?" Bess asked.

"We live outside Seattle," Sumit replied. "Priya works for Amazon, and I teach high school math."

Bess smiled at Lakshmi. "And do you like Las Vegas so far? There's so much to see, right?"

Lakshmi wrinkled her nose. "It smells like cigarettes," she said. "Mummy said Las Vegas is one big ashtray."

Priya groaned as the three of us erupted in laughter.

"Tell us what you *really* think," George said between chuckles.

"Well." Priya sighed. "To be *honest*, which five-year-olds always are, unfortunately, Las Vegas is not my favorite city. I've been here a few times for girls' trips, and once for a bachelorette party . . . it just feels so manufactured to me. Like, there's so much to look at, but it's like the set of a play, you know? We're in the middle of a desert. There's not a *tropical lagoon* here," she said, gesturing to the pool.

I nodded. "I get it," I said. "Las Vegas has a lot of artifice, and maybe that's what makes it fun for some people. But it's not for everybody."

"Exactly." Priya shrugged. "I mean, I'm not a big gambler, either, so it's never seemed like a very fun place to me. Maybe Sumit likes it better?" She glanced up at him curiously.

"Not really," he said, then laughed. "I think it will be lovely to see Veronica—it's been too long. But perhaps I wouldn't have chosen this location."

Priya glanced around. More guests were arriving, but the happy couple had yet to show. "I'm surprised *Veronica* chose this location, to tell the truth. She's never struck me as a Vegas girl."

Sumit nodded. "Well, her interests have changed since she started dating Xavier."

Priya's lips suddenly twisted into a sour look—but just as quickly, she stopped herself and pasted on a smile. "Oh goodness. *Look*."

She was staring out at the pool. We followed her gaze—and then I heard Bess gasp.

"Oh. My. Word," Bess exclaimed.

She let out a whoop just as I spotted what everyone was staring at. Two people were gliding toward us over the pool, at least ten feet above the surface of the water. It looked like they were flying! But actually, they were wearing strange contraptions that looked like hoverboards connected to a long black tube, strapped to their feet. As I watched a little longer, I realized that the tube seemed to suck water out of the pool and then use it to propel the wearer into the air.

"What *is* that?" I asked, as Max appeared out of nowhere with a smartphone and rushed to the front to film the action.

"No idea," replied Priya, as Bess said, "I think it's called a flyboard? It's an extreme sport. You can try it at Redd Zone—but I wasn't expecting to see it here!"

As the couple approached, I recognized Veronica and Xavier—both beaming inside the helmets they were wearing. All of a sudden, both of them bent their knees, crouched down, and then pushed back up, rocketing themselves around in a somersault! The crowd squealed in disbelief. I glanced at my friends. George shook her head and blurted, "What on *earth*? That looked really hard!"

Bess nodded, laughing. "They must have been practicing for weeks!"

Max ran up to the edge of the pool, and Veronica and Max headed toward him first, adjusting the flyboards so they slowly descended to the level of the water, then entered with a *sploosh*! They came back up, and we couldn't quite hear what they were saying as he asked them questions and filmed everything with the phone, but there was lots of laughter and whooping, and at the end I could hear Xavier shout, "Check it out today at the Redd Zone! Live life to the *fullest*!"

I glanced back at my friends and noticed that Priya was frowning. She didn't look happy about any of this.

"Of course he's filming it for social media," she muttered.

Before I could wonder why Priya seemed annoyed,

the crowd of guests—which had filled out a lot while we were chatting with Priya and her family—started pushing toward Veronica and Xavier.

We followed along, but it quickly became clear that *everyone* wanted to chat with the happy couple, and maybe ask them more about the flyboarding. Rather than wait in a big crowd, Bess, George, and I decided to split off and check out the refreshments. We grabbed fruity mocktails at the bar and filled up plates of pupu-platter-style appetizers, then settled around a high table to eat.

"Hey!" George called as Max appeared at the next table, staring out at the water as he pensively sipped a beer. Now that the big entrance was over, he seemed to be without a job, waiting for Xavier and Veronica to greet all their guests. "Want to join us? We're friendly."

Max smiled and walked over, and we all made introductions.

"Oh, that's right," Max said with a smile. He was a little shorter than Xavier, with bushier eyebrows that shaded lighter brown eyes, but they still looked a lot alike. "Veronica's told me about you. It was super nice of you to help with babysitting at the ceremony."

"Are you kidding? Free trip to Vegas?" George laughed. "*And* I get to watch my favorite cousin get married? Twist my arm!"

Max smiled, but just as suddenly as it appeared on his face, his smile seemed to dim. He was looking back at the water now—but toward the beach, where Xavier and Veronica had now taken off their flyboarding contraptions. Both of them were decked out in Redd Zone–branded leggings and bodysuits, and somewhere along the way they'd picked up Redd Zone baseball caps. As we all watched, Xavier took the arm of one of the guests and helped her step onto his now-empty flyboard. Then he helped her strap it on.

"Wait—do the guests get to flyboard too?" Bess asked.

Max nodded. "Oh, yes." For a moment, he looked completely exhausted, but then he looked at Bess and smiled. "Xavier insisted. It was very expensive and complicated to get all the permits and insurance together, but he thinks having people try some of our sports and posting the videos to Redd Zone's social media will really blow us up."

George raised an eyebrow. "You don't sound like you agree," she said.

Max turned away from the flyboarding scene, faced us again, and sighed. "It's . . . Well. Like I said. It's expensive. And complicated. And maybe I don't buy into the whole social media effect in the way that Xavier does."

"It must be a lot of work for you," I said sympathetically.

"It is." Max nodded. "Xavier is the face of the company. . . . I'm the details guy. So with a lot of these things, I'm letting my faith in my brother override my gut feeling. He *does* understand social media better than I do. And he *is* a good salesperson," he added. "Maybe he's right, and we'll reach all kinds of new customers we wouldn't have been able to find otherwise."

Bess looked thoughtful. "Is Redd Zone doing okay?" she asked.

Max stared at her. He looked almost offended. "Of course!" he said. "Why do you ask?"

"Oh." Bess shook her head. "Sorry, it's just—you said this is expensive, but Xavier thinks it will bring in new customers. I thought maybe you *needed* . . ." She shrugged, letting her voice trail off.

Max was shaking his head now. "Not at all," he said. "No, we have a very strong customer base. But it never hurts to try to grow your business." He turned away again, looking back at the beach. Then he put down his beer. "Excuse me," he said. "I should really be filming all this."

He pulled his phone from his pocket and, raising it in front of him, began running toward the action in the pool.

The party continued, the three of us mingling with all the other guests as different people cycled in to try flyboarding, until finally, an hour or so later, we stood before the bride- and groom-to-be.

"*Cuzzies!*" Veronica squealed, smiling a huge smile as she pulled Bess and George in for simultaneous hugs.

"I'm so glad you made it! And Nancy, thank you so much for coming. It means so much to have you all here!"

George grinned, bumping Veronica's shoulder with her own. "There's no place we would rather be!"

As she, Bess, and Veronica continued to chat, Xavier held his hand out to me politely, smiling as he looked directly at me. "I'm Xavier," he said. "I think we met at the barbecue, didn't we?"

"Nancy," I said, smiling back as I shook his hand. "I'm a good friend of Bess and George."

"It's great to meet you, Nancy," Xavier said with a nod. He had a nice smile—kind and genuine and surprisingly humble for someone who seemed to have such a big personality. "Are you enjoying Vegas so far?"

I nodded. "It's—I mean, we haven't been here long, but it's like nowhere else I've ever been." My mind flashed back to Priya's ashtray comment, but that wasn't my impression of Las Vegas—not so far, anyway. It seemed like a playground, almost, a place to forget your troubles and have fun.

Xavier nodded earnestly. "I love Vegas," he said.

"It's a fantasy, but the best kind, you know? And as an extreme-sports guy, I'm always thinking of what I can jump off, or rappel down." He laughed. "You know, the Strip has endless possibilities!"

I nodded. "Like your plans for the wedding?" I asked. "Are you nervous at all about BASE jumping off the rooftop at the Soar?"

Xavier shook his head. "Not '*nervous*,'" he replied. "I like to say '*amped*' instead. All those butterflies in your stomach, your heart pounding, quick breathing? Humans are trained to see that as a bad thing—oh, it's your body telling you not to do what you're about to do. But what if it's the opposite? What if it's your body *coming alive*?"

I swallowed. I'd never really thought of it that way before.

Xavier gestured behind him to the beach. "Are you going to try the flyboard?"

I shook my head automatically. "Oh, no—"

Xavier held up his hand to stop me, then smiled encouragingly. "Let me guess. It's *not for you*?"

I stared at him. That had been exactly what I was about to say.

He nodded. "I'm not making fun of you. I just find that a lot of people say that when I mention extreme sports."

I cleared my throat. "I've just never been a—"

"—daredevil?" Xavier joined in to finish my sentence with me.

I winced, though privately, I wondered what Xavier would say if he knew what kinds of crazy risks I'd taken to solve a case. The difference was, those risks seemed *necessary*, at least at the time. I wasn't the type to take risks just *because*. "You really think you've got a read on me, huh?"

He chuckled good-naturedly. "I think . . . well, give me a minute here. I think a lot of people say they're not daredevils, and believe that about themselves. But I also think it's a way for people to put themselves in a box and wall themselves out of experiences that might challenge them."

My mouth dropped open. "But that's—"

He nodded again. "Condescending, I know. It sounds that way. But I don't mean it that way." He put a hand on my shoulder and gestured to the beach, where another party guest was just going up on the flyboard. "Let me ask you this. How do you know this isn't for you without trying it? Is there any part of you that can imagine trying it and having a really good time?"

I watched for a moment. The woman who was flyboarding looked like she'd never tried it before, based on her nervous expression, the way she was biting her lip, the way she seemed to have trouble controlling her trajectory. But within seconds, she was laughing, then screaming to her friend. There was still fear in her eyes, but as she began to move around the pool, it was joined by something else: pure joy.

I took in a breath and tried to imagine myself trying it. I imagined what it would feel like to step onto the board, to get all strapped in, to put on the helmet, to cast a terrified look at Max, who was helping the flyboarders get going while Xavier mingled with the other guests. I imagined pressing the button or whatever to push myself up into the air, and then careening around on a jet of water—

Oh, wait. There it was. In my imagination, I was screaming and laughing in delight, just the way the woman I'd been watching was now.

When I looked at Xavier, he was already smiling. He'd seen it all on my face. "Why not try it?" he asked with a casual shrug. "If you hate it, after all, you never have to do it again. And when else will you have the chance?"

When *would* I have the chance? It was true; I didn't go to extreme-sports weddings every day. I shook my head, unable to believe I was about to say this. Before I could stop them, I let the words out: "Okay. I'll try it."

Beside me, Bess overheard and squealed. "*What?* Nancy!"

"Don't talk her out of it!" Xavier said, putting his arm around my shoulders and leading me toward the beach. "Ladies and gentlemen! We have another first-time flyboarder on our hands!"

Before I could think better of it, we arrived at the little sand beach. The woman I'd been watching was still going, laughing her head off, but the other suit was available, and Max glanced up, pointing from me to it with a questioning look.

"Are you sure, Nancy?" George asked. She and Bess had rushed in behind me.

I looked at my friends, then at Xavier, then at the woman whooping excitedly as she flew over the water.

"I'm sure," I said, looking Max in the eye. "Can you help me suit up?"

He nodded, smiling warmly. "It would be my pleasure."

First I had to borrow a wet suit and go into a little wooden shack to change out of my cocktail attire. Then I had to put on a life jacket and buckle it up. Then it was time to walk out on a dock that led into the deeper part of the pool and get on the board.

As I got closer, I could see that there were boots attached to the board, and that there were actually handholds, too, that strapped onto your arms. *That must be how you control it.* And now that I was about to get into the water, I could see that the hose that seemed to propel the flyboard up was actually attached to a Jet Ski—which was being driven by a woman a little older than me. She waved at me encouragingly, and I waved back.

"You're going to love it!" she yelled.

Max gestured for me to step onto the board and into the boots. I stepped onto the middle of the board with my left foot and inserted my right foot into the boot, then my left. As Max tightened up the straps, I took a deep breath, wondering if I would regret this. Was Xavier some kind of mind-reading wizard? How had he talked me into this? Now that I thought about it, I couldn't even remember what he'd said. How had I, Nancy Drew, master reader of vibes and intentions and sales pitches, fallen under his spell?

Max helped me put on the handholds, then produced a helmet and slipped it onto my head, covering my ears. My hands were attached to the flyboard, so he adjusted the strap under my chin and gave me a cheer-ful nod. "Ready?" he asked.

"Ready," I replied, though I was not sure that I was ready at all.

Here goes nothing. . . .

CHAPTER THREE

~∾~

Flying High

IT TURNS OUT THAT FLYBOARDING STARTS with a really ungraceful fall off the dock into the water. Max encouraged me to keep my legs straight—the legs had to stay straight for the whole ride, unless I wanted to turn—and my head high. The woman on the Jet Ski—Max told me her name was Ruby—fired it up, and Max warned me that I would feel the power in the hose leading to the flyboard. After a few minutes, I could feel the hose getting more tense, and I raised my head, ready to rise up into the air.

It worked!

I gasped as the flyboard sent me up over the water, pausing at about five feet above the pool—a safe level for beginners, Max had told me. I looked around at my friends, who were both cheering like crazy from the shore. Xavier clapped and gave me a thumbs-up.

My legs were stiff with adrenaline and I felt like my heart might beat out of my chest, but I was *doing it*! I was flying, sort of! I leaned forward, trying to nudge myself forward, and began gliding across the water. I leaned back, pointing my toes skyward, and went up.

"Omigosh!" I screamed. "You guys—I'm flyboarding!"

The sun had set by now, and the lights of the Strip at dusk reflected in the pool were absolutely gorgeous. I experimented with going back and forth, then bent my right knee to turn right. I soon realized that if I kept one knee bent, I could keep spiraling in a helix shape. The lights of the Strip blurred around me and I felt like I was in a dream.

"Nancy!"

Oh no. I was tilting—my helix pointing dangerously

toward the water. I tried to straighten my leg, but I was too late. I crashed through the surface of the water and quickly closed my mouth and eyes. Max had told me not to panic if I hit the water, that I might have my head under for as much as two seconds, but that the vest, helmet, and board itself all floated. Sure enough, it was uncomfortable, and water got up my nose, but before I could blink, my head broke the surface again. I tried to lie flat, and soon was back in the position I'd started from.

Bess and George were still cheering, and Xavier yelled, "Way to keep your cool, Nancy!"

Max called from the beach, "Would you like to try going up again?"

I pondered. Normally, Nancy Drew would not go up again. Nancy Drew would pat herself on the back for trying something new and call it a day. But I was learning that trying new things sometimes led to great rewards.

"Yes!" I shouted. "Let's try it again."

So I got up on the flyboard again, and soon the

lights were swirling around me once more as I experienced what it was like to fly on the Las Vegas strip. For a while it was like everything around me faded into the distance, and it was just me and the lights and the flyboard and the water. I could feel my heart pounding, and I could hear my wild, uncontrollable laughter.

I was so glad I'd done it. So glad I'd tried. Maybe Xavier *was* some kind of wizard—a good one.

After a little while I decided to come down and give someone else a turn. I had to plunge into the water again, but did as I'd done before and let the equipment float me back to the surface. It wasn't as scary this time. And soon I was back on the beach. Bess and George ran toward me and cheered. Max helped me up and began unstrapping the handholds, and then we both unlaced and loosened the boots.

As soon as I was free, Bess and George ran in for a hug. "Careful!" I shouted, laughing. "I'm soaked!"

"I can't believe you did that," Bess said, shaking her head admiringly. "Was it amazing? It looked amazing."

"It was pretty amazing," I admitted, glancing over at

Xavier, who was chatting with a few guests at a high table. I waved and called, "Thanks for getting me up there!"

He smiled that million-watt smile that probably made him an effective salesperson. "You did great!" he shouted, then gave me a thumbs-up and turned back to his conversation.

By the time I'd changed out of the wet suit, the party was winding down. George reminded us that she had a full day of sightseeing planned for tomorrow. So it seemed like the right time to start the walk back up the Strip to the Soar.

As we were saying goodbye to the happy couple, Xavier nudged me and smiled encouragingly. "So if *that* was amazing," he said quietly, "think about all the other things you talk yourself out of trying that might be amazing."

I huffed out a laugh, shaking my head. "I'm not BASE jumping off the Soar, if that's what you're implying. You're on your own there."

He nodded. "Fair enough. Baby steps. But it was fun, right?"

"It was really fun."

And later, when I was cozied up in my pj's in bed, with my eyes closed, I kept going back to the feeling of gliding over the water with the lights of the Strip all around me. It had felt like nothing I'd ever experienced before. And I was so glad I'd done it.

The next day Bess held up a compact mirror in the back of a taxi and frowned at her reflection. "Is it totally obvious I'm sunburned?"

George and I exchanged an awkward glance. After a long day of sightseeing in the hot desert sun, Bess's cheeks, nose, and forehead were roughly the color of the flesh of a guava. It was kind of obvious. But George and I were pretty pink too.

"You look fine," I said quickly.

George glanced out the window at a wide expanse of desert, brush, and rock formations. "So this is what the land around Vegas is like, huh? Pretty different from the Strip."

"You can say that again," Bess said, slipping the

mirror back into her purse with a sigh. "Where is this place, anyway? This doesn't look like the kind of area where a restaurant big enough to host a rehearsal dinner would pop up."

Mario, our taxi driver, cleared his throat. "The address you gave me isn't for a restaurant," he explained. "It's . . . well. It's kind of in the middle of nowhere."

Bess, George, and I exchanged weird looks.

"Do you think this is like the engagement barbecue?" George asked, eyebrows furrowed. "Are we going to be expected to—I dunno, jump out of a plane or something?"

"Ooh!" Bess raised her hand. "Yes, please! I'd volunteer."

I cleared my throat. "Well, I get the feeling *something* unusual is happening at this rehearsal dinner. But I'm not taking part tonight. Remember, George—we're on babysitting duty."

George nodded, lifting up a bag of coloring books, crayons, and small toys we'd put together that afternoon. "I'm kind of looking forward to it, to be honest."

She nudged Bess. "You be the social butterfly. Nancy and I will make small talk with the *Peppa Pig* crowd."

Bess frowned. "Wait, I have feelings about *Peppa Pig*. Why do they call a shopping cart a shopping trolley?"

"Why do you watch *Peppa Pig*, Bess?" I asked.

She glanced at me. "It's on all the time, Nancy. And I love the accents."

"Here we are," Mario interrupted as he pulled into a dusty driveway on the left that led to a parking lot for a small park. And sure enough—right there in the desert, overlooking a rocky cliff, a few rustic picnic tables were set with dinner plates and beautiful white roses. A taco truck was parked nearby, and a couple of bartenders were pouring drinks from a small bar set up just beyond the truck.

It looked like more guests had arrived over the course of the day. I saw several faces I didn't recognize from the cocktail get-together the night before. Deanna was also there with her family, and Priya waved at us from a table where she sat with Sumit, Lakshmi, and Max.

Bess paid Mario as George and I walked over to collect Lakshmi. "Hey, are you ready to have some fun with us?" George asked with a warm smile. "We have all the best coloring books and a hundred-twenty box of Crayola. Plus—not to brag—*bubbles*."

Lakshmi's eyes widened. "Bubbles?" she asked excitedly.

"*So many* bubbles," I promised.

Lakshmi looked back at Priya, who nodded encouragingly. "You go and have fun, baby," she cooed, then turned to us. "Thank you, girls—I'm looking forward to having grown-up fun!"

"Me too," Sumit agreed. "Vegas with a five-year-old is . . . well, different than I remember."

We all laughed, and George took Lakshmi's hand. "Come on, kiddo. Let's go find some other kids to play with."

After a few minutes, George and I had collected Deanna's kids, Miranda and Luka, and settled them at a picnic table with the coloring books and toys. We were chatting happily about what we'd all done that day, our favorite parts of Vegas, and the pool at the Soar. The dinner service was starting, but we hung back and waited for the long line at the taco truck to go down. Most of the adult guests were waiting to order food, and Max was running around the whole area, capturing the party on his phone for Redd Zone's social media.

George glanced up from the page she was coloring and followed my gaze to Max. "I wonder if he ever gets a break," she murmured.

Max did seem to be working hard. Sweat had broken out on his forehead, and he was aiming his phone and calling questions to guests with a sort of manic intensity. Everyone was responding with good humor, and the mood at the party was chill, but Max seemed very intent on getting a certain kind of content.

"Yeah, I hope he gets to relax and enjoy a taco at some point," I agreed.

That was when I noticed a tall figure standing behind our table in the shadows. He looked to be about Xavier's age, but I couldn't see his face because he was as still as a statue, facing away from us over the cliff. I glanced away, but when I looked back a few minutes later, he was still there.

Weird. I nudged George and pointed. "You know that guy?"

George looked and frowned, shaking her head. "I don't think he was at the Polynesian yesterday."

"What's he doing?" I wondered out loud. *Why wasn't he moving? Why was he just staring into the darkness? Why was he so near our table?*

George shrugged. She met my eye, and I could see my awkwardness reflected in her gaze: *Should we be concerned?*

"He's a wedding guest, right?" I asked, feeling silly.

George looked back over at him, then shrugged again. "Probably? What else would he be doing here?"

Good question. I stood up from the picnic table. "I'm just going to go say hello."

The sky was darkening, and already sunset colors were flooding the sky—in the other direction. This guy was staring out into the gathering shadows. As I got closer, I could see that he was dressed much more casually than the other guests, in jeans and a hoodie. He had brown hair that was buzzed on the sides and long on top. I still couldn't see his face, though.

"Hi," I said loudly, stopping just a few feet behind him. "I'm Nancy. How do you know Veronica and Xavier?"

For a few seconds, the man didn't move or acknowledge my question, and I could feel the hairs standing up on the back of my neck. *Who is this guy?* But then he slowly turned and looked at me. He had blue, sort of watery eyes, pale skin, and an amused-looking smirk. "Hi, Nancy. I'm Arlo." He held out his hand.

"Hi," I said, shaking it, though I was puzzled. *Arlo the wedding guest? Arlo the creepy dude who's here for nefarious purposes?* "You're here for the rehearsal dinner?"

He let out a hard laugh. "Oh yeah, sorry. I'm an old friend of Xavier's."

"How old?" I asked, wanting as much detail as I could get now.

"We met in middle school," Arlo replied. "We were best buddies all through high school. But that was a million years ago. Xavier was very different then."

"Different how?"

Arlo shook his head. "Oh, you know. Not a business tycoon yet? Not Mr. Extreme Sports?" He smiled, but whether it was warm or cold, amused or upset, I couldn't read. Even facing the sunset, as he was now, much of his face was angled so as to still be in shadow. "Actually," he began, and his voice got deeper, "we talked about going into business together back in high school. We were going to sell sports gear. Try to make a deal with the high school to do varsity jackets, that kind of thing. But then . . ."

He trailed off, and I waited, wondering if he was going to continue. He was looking over my head now, I guessed at the sunset.

"Then . . . ?" I prompted.

He shook his head again, then looked back at me. "It wasn't Xavier's fault. I went through a tough time, ended up in prison."

"Oh, wow," I said, not sure how to respond. "I'm sorry."

"Don't be. It was my fault. My mistake. But I paid for it, I did my time, and here I am." He gestured around us. "Three weeks ago, I get out and one of the first pieces of mail I get is Xavier's wedding invitation. Getting married in Vegas. Can you believe it?"

I nodded. "It's . . . pretty crazy, right? Was Xavier into all this extreme-sports stuff when you knew him in high school?"

"No, all we were into was getting in trouble," Arlo scoffed. But he was better at not getting caught." He looked over at the rest of the party, nodding toward the bride- and groom-to-be. "Good for them, though."

"Right," I said, still feeling slightly uneasy. "Good for them. Well." I looked around. "It was really nice to meet you. I think—I'd better get back and make sure the kids get some dinner. My friend George and I— she's Veronica's cousin—we're babysitting tonight and at the ceremony tomorrow. My other friend, Bess, she's Veronica's other cousin and she's a bridesmaid."

Arlo nodded. "I met Bess during the rehearsal earlier tonight."

I startled. "You're in the wedding party?"

He smiled then, a real smile. "Can you believe it?" he asked. "I guess you never forget your real friends."

An hour or so later, we'd eaten all the tacos we could (they were delicious) and the kids were entertaining themselves with the bubble kits we'd brought. Arlo had disappeared into the party, though there was something about him, and about our conversation, that still felt awkward to me. Max had finally put down the phone and had some dinner, but now I saw him passing the phone to Deanna as he picked up a cordless microphone and stood up from his table.

"Excuse me?" he asked, flicking on the mic and tapping on its surface. "Can I have everyone's attention, please? It's time for us to toast the happy couple."

"Uh-oh," I heard, barely audible, from George.

"What?" I asked, turning to her. "You're afraid he's going to say something embarrassing about Xavier?"

She looked around and shook her head. "It's not that," she whispered to me. "Have you ever been to a traditional rehearsal dinner where everyone makes a toast? It can go on for *hours*."

"Everyone has to toast?" I asked.

"Shhh," she replied. "I think Max is starting."

Sure enough, Max was talking about when he and Xavier were kids and Xavier had a crush on their babysitter. He detailed all the silly things little Xavier had done to make the babysitter notice him, leading to him taking her out on what he understood to be a "date." Hijinks ensued. It was a pretty funny story, and soon the party guests were cracking up. Even Xavier seemed to be enjoying it. But then Max pivoted. "And since then," he said, "I've never seen Xavier so hyperfocused, so totally in love with a woman . . . until you, Veronica." He lifted his glass. "So I'd like to toast my brother and the spectacular woman he loves. May your life together include reaching the highest peaks, experiencing the biggest thrills, and never forgetting that the most exciting adventure is experienced with the person you love."

"Hear! Hear!"

We all raised our glasses, and a few people applauded. After we'd all sipped our drinks, Deanna stood up and took the mic.

"My big sister," she began, her eyes large and teary. "I've looked up to you my whole life."

Deanna's speech was short and sentimental. She talked about introducing Xavier to Veronica, and how she knew immediately that they were made for each other. She talked about how Xavier had brought out parts of her sister she never knew and had helped her experience things Deanna never would have imagined.

"I love you both so much," she finished. "I hope you have a long and happy life together, and that our kids get to play together in Mami and Papi's backyard."

We all raised our glasses and drank. Then a woman I hadn't seen before took the mic and introduced herself as Xavier's aunt.

George was right. The toasts went on and on, and began to blend together. Veronica's sorority sister.

Xavier's college roommate. Xavier's first boss. Everyone was so loving, so complimentary, and so happy for the couple. I was carefully watching the kids as it grew darker, wondering how much more good behavior they had in them before boredom and sleepiness took over.

After a half hour or so, Priya stood up. She seemed a little wobbly, like she'd been enjoying her champagne for a lot longer than the toasts had been going on. She looked straight at Veronica and called her a sister, telling stories from their years at college about how devoted they had both been to each other. "You are perfect just as you are," Priya said earnestly, leaning in toward Veronica, who looked a little uncomfortable. "*Don't change* for anybody, please, Ronny. You don't have to do anything you don't want to do."

There was silence for a moment, Priya's warning hanging in the air. Was it a blessing or a curse? No one seemed to know how to react until Veronica raised her glass high, said, "I love you, Yaya," and took a big sip. That seemed to break the spell and give the rest of the party guests permission to do the same.

Still, George nudged me. "What do you think *that* was about?" she whispered.

"If I were to guess," I whispered back, noting that Veronica and Xavier were also whispering fiercely to each other, "I would say Priya is not a big Xavier fan."

More toasts followed. Veronica's coworker. A cousin I didn't know. And then a familiar face stepped up to the mic.

"Arlo," I whispered to George, who nodded. I'd told her a little bit about my conversation with him earlier.

"I've known Xavier since we were kids," Arlo said. "In some ways, he hasn't changed at all. In other ways, I barely recognize him."

The crowd grew quiet, not seeming to know how to take Arlo's words. But Xavier was watching his old friend warmly.

"Xavier is the absolute best. The life of every party, the charmer who can win over your mother. He always has a dream, and he'll do whatever it takes to reach it. I love you, dude, even if I could never count on you for anything. Have a happy life!"

As with Priya's toast, the crowd was silent for a little while after Arlo finished speaking. *I could never count on you for anything?* George mouthed to me, and yeah, it seemed a little harsh for a rehearsal dinner speech. But Xavier didn't seem angry at all—he was laughing, raising his glass high. Arlo walked over to him, and they hugged it out. Soon the rest of the party seemed to follow Xavier's lead, drinking and laughing. Arlo faded back into the crowd.

I tried not to stare at him. There was something about the guy that set me on edge.

Yet more toasts followed. Soon there was just a tiny ring of orange on the horizon where the sun had disappeared. Candles were lit on each table, and fairy lights came on around the taco truck and the bar. But mostly, it was dark.

When finally, a toast was finished and no one came up to claim the microphone after, Xavier stood up to enthusiastic applause. I noticed Max take his phone and begin filming again.

"Thank you," he said. "I'm a lucky man, because tomorrow, I get to marry the love of my life. Not many people can say that. And Veronica knows how I feel about her, because I tell her every day. But even so, baby: I love you to the moon and back. There's no one else I would ever want beside me as copilot on this crazy ride called life."

Cheers from the audience, and applause. Xavier leaned in to kiss Veronica, and she happily accepted.

"And now!" Xavier yelled into the mic when they'd finished. "In celebration of our love, Veronica and I are going to do something *amazing*—we're BASE jumping off this cliff in wingsuits, son!"

His announcement was met with a confusion of sounds. Some cheers. Some gasps. Priya yelled, *"What?"* in a not-very-enthusiastic voice.

Max put down his phone. "We're still doing that?" he asked Xavier.

Xavier looked from Veronica to his brother,

confused. "Of course we are! This whole night was planned around it, bro."

Max gestured to the cliff, cloaked in darkness. "It's much darker than we'd planned."

Xavier shrugged. "So? The toasts went long—and that's fine. Veronica and I, we felt a lot of love tonight. Maybe it's later than we'd planned on doing the jump. But if you know what you're doing, it doesn't matter."

Max didn't say anything, but he stared at his brother challengingly. Xavier stared right back. After a few uncomfortable seconds, Max shook his head and sighed.

"All right. But we need to hurry to catch the light that's left."

Xavier, Veronica, and Max all jumped up and hurried to the edge of the cliff, where I could now see that equipment had been stowed in some brush. They began putting on gear as I turned to George, eyes wide. Bess, who had been sitting at another table, stood and walked over to ours. She had a perturbed look on her face.

I heard Lakshmi shrieking, "Not fair! That's *my* bubble wand!" as Bess leaned in.

"Are we . . . happy about this?" she asked, gesturing vaguely at the cliff.

George turned to look at Veronica and Xavier, biting her lip. "Mmmm—undecided?" she replied.

"I don't do enough BASE jumping to know," I said. "Is doing it in the dark dangerous?"

"It doesn't seem like a *great* idea," Bess murmured.

We were all looking over at Max and the marrieds-to-be now. Xavier and Veronica had put on these bizarre flight suits, which, yes, had funny wings sewn in between the sleeves and body.

"Do they just—fly on those wings?" I asked. "Should I know what's going on here?"

Bess pointed a finger in the air. "No," she said, "but I know a little about it. I researched the most popular extreme sports after I tried bungee jumping. I guess with a BASE jump using a wingsuit, the suit acts as a sort of hang glider, keeping you aloft as you glide forward. But eventually, you have to deploy a parachute.

And BASE jumping is especially dangerous because the suit only allows you one parachute. There's not a backup, like there is in skydiving."

I shivered. *Too dark, no backup*—none of this sounded good. But Xavier was waving people over, and we joined the other guests in getting to our feet and carefully making our way to the edge of the cliff. I corralled Miranda and Luka while George took Lakshmi by the hand. I could tell from the look in George's eyes that she felt the same way I did: desperate for this to end safely, so we could all go back to worrying about the wedding tomorrow.

Max had set up a few bright lights that lit up the area Xavier and Veronica would be jumping from, if not much of the drop beyond. As we moved closer to the cliff, I couldn't help pushing the kids back and stepping up to peer over the edge. Immediately, icy cold panic slid up my spine. The drop was at least five hundred feet. In the distance were a few rock formations, and the desert floor was studded with brush and a few spiky trees. But mostly, what I saw was a dark, gaping maw. If you fell, you would not walk away.

"Are we ready?" Xavier yelled.

"Never been more ready!" Veronica shouted back.

Max raised his phone again, ready to capture the jump for posterity.

"Let's count down," Xavier said. "We're losing daylight, so only from three. Everyone ready? Three . . . two . . ."

I felt my chest clench with panic as the whole crowd shouted, "One!" and Veronica and Xavier stepped off the cliff—and leaned into the darkness.

It was hard to keep sight of the couple over the darkening desert, but every so often I could see the blue-white of their suits as they seemed to glide weightlessly on currents of air. Little by little, they descended more and more, until finally one jumper sent up a parachute that filled and slowed their fall with a loud *poof!*

"That's Veronica!" Bess cried. "Hooray, she's safe!"

But what was Xavier doing? He was getting closer and closer to the ground, and he seemed to be struggling, his arms working furiously at something. . . .

"Oh no," George whispered. "Is the parachute jammed?"

"No!" Bess cried.

My heart began pounding faster and faster as Xavier's figure kept falling. He was moving so fast—too fast to survive without a parachute. Instinctively I took the kids by the shoulder and gently pulled them back from the edge of the cliff.

"Do you guys have bubbles left?" I asked, fishing around in my pockets to distract them. But I felt sick with dread.

Crash! A loud sound emanated from the desert floor.

"Oh, thank goodness!" Bess cried. "He landed in a tree!"

"But is he all right?" asked George. "Can you survive that kind of fall?"

Bess was quiet for a moment. "I'm not sure," she said finally. "He isn't moving. . . ."

CHAPTER FOUR

A Night to Remember

"CAN YOU WATCH THE KIDS?" I ASKED George, and without even thinking I pulled out my phone, turned on the flashlight, and peered over the cliff again. There was a walking path, almost but not quite wide enough to be a road, that zigzagged along the rock face to the bottom. Lighting my way with my phone, I started hightailing it down to the desert floor.

I wasn't alone. Max was bolting ahead of me, and Deanna's husband, Eduardo, ran behind. Deanna was screaming from the top of the ledge. *"Is he all right? Ay . . ."*

"I know CPR," I puffed quickly to Max as I caught up with him.

He turned and glanced at me with surprise. "Good," he said simply. "Me too."

Meanwhile, Veronica had landed safely and was also running toward the tree where Xavier had crashed. "Babe? Are you okay? *Babe!*" Her voice was becoming increasingly desperate. Was Xavier conscious? I couldn't tell.

Finally we reached the bottom of the cliff and ran toward the tree, a good two hundred yards away. Normally, I'd be winded by now, but adrenaline was keeping me going. I could feel the tension and dread in the air. *Is this wedding going to turn into a tragedy?*

But when I was about ten yards from the tree, I heard it: the sound that changed everything. A moan coming from the branches of the tree.

"Oh, man," Xavier groaned, and the branches shifted as he seemed to move. "That . . . hurt."

Veronica's eyes widened with relief. "Babe, can you hear me? Are you conscious?"

He moaned again. "I think I'm okay," he called. "Just . . . banged up."

I drew up to Veronica's side and heard her let out a sigh of relief. Max was behind me now, already on his phone. "Okay . . . yes . . . we're in Frick Canyon Park. Yes, he seems to be conscious. Should we try to move him or . . . ? Okay, okay, got it. Yeah, I don't see a road down here. . . ."

I glanced at Veronica a little awkwardly. She didn't know me well, but I still grabbed her hand and gave it a squeeze. She looked at me.

"He'll be okay," I said gently.

She nodded, but her eyes still looked troubled. "I know. I know. It'll be okay," she replied.

After that, things seemed to move really fast. It was only a few minutes before we heard a helicopter moving in from behind us. It got louder and louder until it touched down in a clearing several yards beyond the tree. From there we just tried to stay out of the paramedics' way as they carefully dislodged Xavier from the tree and strapped him to a gurney.

Veronica hovered nearby as the EMTs did a quick exam and checked Xavier's vital signs. "No major internal injuries," one of them, a Black woman about Deanna's age, told Veronica. "Looks like your boyfriend was very lucky."

"Fiancé," Xavier corrected with a groan. "We're getting married tomorrow."

The EMT frowned. "*Are* you?" she asked. "Let's see what the doctors say. We need to get you to the hospital for a full exam."

They wheeled the gurney into the helicopter, and Veronica darted in to sit next to Xavier.

"What hospital are you going to?" Max asked.

"Grace Memorial," the EMT responded. "If you drive, he'll already be there. Just ask for him at the front desk."

She shut the door, and within seconds, the helicopter's blades began whirring again. The copter lifted into the air and began slowly, then quickly, flying back in the direction of the city.

Max, Eduardo, and I were left in the dark. The sun

had fully set now. I looked back at the cliff with dread. "Now I guess . . . we start the climb back up?" I asked, pulling out my phone again.

Max shook his head. "Not so fast," he said, pulling his own flashlight out of his pocket. He walked a little ways back toward the cliff and then disappeared into some brush. I heard an engine start up, and then an ATV squealed out of the brush, Max in the driver's seat.

"Hop in," he said with a nod. "This is how Veronica and Xavier were going to get back up to the park."

Eduardo and I looked at each other and shrugged.

"That looks a lot better than the climb," Eduardo said.

We got in, me in the passenger seat and Eduardo in the back. The ATV bumped and growled up the path, and I held on hard. When we reached the top, George and Bess greeted me eagerly and I filled them in on what I'd heard.

"Everybody," Max yelled, "I'm happy to tell you that Xavier is conscious and his vitals look good. He's on his way to the hospital now. We can all head back to the hotel, and I'll update you if there are any changes to the plans tomorrow. I know Veronica and Xavier will do everything they can to pull off the wedding if it's possible!"

Murmurs ran through the crowd, and slowly, everyone started heading back toward the parking lot. George got on her phone and ordered us an Uber.

We were weirdly silent. "I don't know what to say," I said finally.

Bess and George exchanged glances, and Bess shrugged. "Me either," she admitted. "Still processing, I guess."

Within half an hour we were back at the Soar. The bright lights and cacophonous sounds of the casino felt overwhelming after the quiet of the desert. We headed to the elevators, but once we were inside a car, zooming toward our floor, George shook her head.

"There's no way I'm going to be able to sleep," she said. "I'm too keyed up."

"Me too," Bess agreed.

"Me too," I said with a nod. "Want to get a soda or something and talk about it?"

We decided to check out the Sky Bar, a bar/café that was just below the roof-deck where Veronica and Xavier were scheduled to be married the next day. It had a gorgeous view of the Strip and a little outdoor observation deck, but we walked right by it and settled inside at a high table near a window. George ordered a large fries—"I'm comfort eating, you guys"—and we all got Cokes.

After the order was placed, we still sat in silence for a while. It wasn't until the drinks came and we'd snacked on a few fries that Bess broke it.

"Guys," she said finally, running her hands over her hair, "if Veronica's parachute had jammed instead of Xavier's, George and I could have lost our cousin."

George grunted. "Yeah, and Veronica almost lost her fiancé—the night before their wedding."

"It's awful," I agreed.

We all shook our heads.

Bess sighed. "I've had a lot of fun trying out extreme sports with Veronica and Xavier, but now I wonder if the risk is worth the reward. I feel terrible that this happened. Were the conditions too dangerous tonight? Should we have tried harder to stop it?"

George snorted. "Yeah, cuz, because if there's anyone a big group of adults listen to, it's teenagers."

Bess shook her head and frowned. "I just feel like . . . everyone knew it was a bad idea," she said. "Everyone except Veronica and Xavier. We just sat there and watched!"

"It seemed like they really wanted to do it," I said gently.

George pursed her lips. "Xavier did, anyway."

I shrugged. "I mean, Veronica seemed excited too. Although, when we were at the bottom of the canyon, when Xavier was in the tree . . ."

"Yes?" Bess asked, raising an eyebrow.

I paused, then shook my head. "I don't know. She seemed upset, but of course she did. She wasn't sure Xavier would be okay."

Bess sighed through her nose. We were all quiet for another minute or so.

"Do you think he's pressuring her?" Bess asked, looking at George. "We've known Veronica since we were babies. She never even wanted to jump off the high dive at her community pool. But now she's all about BASE jumping and bungee jumping and"—she waved her arms—"all kinds of whackadoo things."

George tilted her head to the side. "It kind of seems like Priya thinks so," she remarked. "Remember that toast?"

Bess nodded. "Don't change for anyone? Something like that? The '*anyone*' was obviously Xavier."

I lifted my Coke to my lips for a long sip, then took a deep breath. "Guys, Veronica seems like a smart woman. Is it even fair to think Xavier *could* pressure her? She seems totally capable of deciding what she wants to do. And people *do* change."

I was thinking about my own time on the flyboard—not something Nancy Drew would have done normally. But I'd made my own decision, and I didn't regret it. Why should we believe that Veronica wasn't making her own decisions in the same way?

George looked thoughtful. "You're right, Nancy," she said after a few seconds. "I trust Veronica. So if she trusts Xavier, I do too."

Bess looked out the window. "I hope she's okay," she said. "I really hope this all works out, and we get to go to the happy wedding we came for tomorrow." She pulled out her phone. "No text yet about Xavier," she said.

George shrugged. "I guess there's no news yet."

Bess nodded, mindlessly clicking through her phone. I watched her pull up Instagram and quickly swipe through her feed. *"Oh,"* she said suddenly, sitting back in her chair as she stared at the screen.

George glanced at me with a quizzical look. "What is it, cuz?"

Bess took in a slow breath. "Uh . . . I guess there *is* word on Xavier."

She turned on the sound and put the phone down on the table, facing us.

"Hey, hey, hey!"

I stared at the screen. The speaker was Xavier—in a video taken just minutes before, according to the post. He was sitting on a hospital bed in a gown, gesturing with his left hand. His right arm hung lifeless at his side.

"I want to say what's up and a huge thank you to the ER staff here at Grace Memorial in Sin City! Your boy Xavier had a *craaaaaazy* accident tonight, guys! But I'm not just going to tell you about it—I'll show you." The video quickly cut to footage taken from the rehearsal dinner of Xavier and Veronica kissing before making the BASE jump off the top of the cliff. It followed Xavier through the jump, as he was gliding down, and finally as he seemed to struggle with the parachute. Watching the video, I realized he'd been screaming as he crashed into the tree, and then his screams were abruptly silenced.

I could feel my heart beating wildly, even though I knew he was okay. He'd survived.

The video on Instagram abruptly cut back to

Xavier in the hospital. "Do I have regrets?" he asked, and laughed. "Maybe I *should*, dude—but the truth is, I feel amazing! They think I broke my arm, so I may have to bag on the BASE jump tomorrow, but I'm psyched to marry that girl! Mostly because I know we feel the same way about life—that you have to push the limits! Live life to the *extreme*! And when I get back to Chicago, we're going to take Redd Zone to the *next level*!"

He punched his fist at the camera, and the video ended.

Bess pressed a button to put her phone to sleep as the three of us stared at one another in disbelief.

"He posted on *Instagram* already?" George asked finally.

"He made it sound like a *good* thing, almost," Bess said, looking incredulous. "Like, oh, I almost died—but that's what happens when you live life to the fullest! Let's do it some *more*!"

"It's like he's using his accident to advertise his business," I said slowly, not wanting to believe it. "But is that responsible? He *did* take unnecessary risks tonight. And he got lucky, but he could have died."

Bess frowned. "I don't like it," she said. "I want to like Xavier, but . . . this weirds me out."

"Me too," George agreed, taking the last fry. She looked uncomfortable. "You don't think he, like . . . *planned* it, do you?"

"George!" Bess looked at her in alarm.

George held up her hands. "I just . . . he's using it to market his business. You're right, it's crazy. But he clearly thinks it's going to play with his customers."

"He *almost died*," I pointed out. "Even a daredevil like Xavier wouldn't risk that much to sell more bungee jumps. Would he?"

Bess and George were quiet for a few seconds before George admitted, "Probably not. And the owner having this huge accident might make potential Redd Zone customers nervous, anyway. You're right. Ignore me."

Still, we all seemed to feel unsettled. I said I was getting tired, and Bess asked for the bill.

"It's been a long night," Bess said as we walked back to the elevators a few minutes later. "I'm really glad I'm here with you two."

"Me too," I echoed.

We looked at George, but she didn't seem to be paying attention to us. She was leaning back to stare out the window at the outdoor observation deck, a look of confusion on her face.

"Is that . . . Veronica?"

We all turned toward the window. Sure enough, a lone figure who looked an awful lot like Veronica was standing against the railing, looking down at the Strip.

Bess scrunched up her brows. "She's not with Xavier?"

"Maybe he's back too," I suggested. "Maybe they set his arm really fast, or it turned out not to be broken."

George shook her head. "I doubt it. Those things take a while." She paused, squinting. "But I'm pretty sure that's the dress Veronica was wearing at the party."

She looked back at us, and the three of us had a

silent conversation: *Do we go out there? We kind of have to check on her, don't we?*

Bess was the first to push open the door to the observation deck and head out.

It was chilly outside, a cool wind blowing in off the desert. I pulled my wrap closer around me. The observation deck stretched along this whole side of the casino, but it was only ten or so feet deep. We all followed Bess as she walked up to the Veronica figure and put a hand on her shoulder. "Cuz?"

Veronica startled and turned around. "Oh . . . hi," she said. But her eyes looked red and hollow, and she couldn't seem to match her voice to the fake-looking smile she'd pasted on.

"Are you okay?" George asked. "I mean, I'm guessing that wasn't the rehearsal dinner of your dreams. That had to be scary."

Veronica turned her gaze to George, but she barely seemed to absorb what she'd said. "I'm fine. And Xavier is going to be fine. You don't have to worry about me, cuz."

But I wasn't even related to Veronica, and *I* was feeling a little worried about her. Despite what she said, she didn't *look* fine at all. She looked shaken and sad.

"It had to be tough," I said quietly, "seeing Xavier get hurt like that."

Veronica turned to look at me. It was weird, though—I couldn't read anything in her large, dark eyes. It was like she wasn't even fully there. Like we'd interrupted a conversation she was having with herself, and she hadn't fully joined this one.

"He'll be fine," she said simply. "They're setting his arm at the hospital. And his daredevil streak is part of what I love about him."

For a moment, the four of us just stood there awkwardly. Veronica sounded like she was reading this off a card. What was going on with her? I could tell from George's and Bess's concerned looks that they were finding this as strange as I was.

"Well," Bess said finally. "What a relief. I guess we'll see you at the wedding tomorrow, then. We'll let you get some rest."

We said our good nights, but Veronica didn't leave with us. She moved back to the railing and kept staring down at the lights of the Strip.

Bess, George, and I were silent until the elevator doors closed behind us.

"That was weird," Bess said. "I really hope she's okay."

"Me too," I agreed.

George sighed. "I'll be relieved when this wedding is over," she said. "I love Veronica, and I hope she and Xavier are really happy together. But this is all getting a little too *extreme* for me."

CHAPTER FIVE

Here Comes the Bride . . .

"I DON'T KNOW," BESS SAID WITH A SIGH AS she looked into the lighted mirror in Veronica's hotel suite bathroom. "Is it too, like, *Marvelous Mrs. Maisel* or something?"

It was the next day, just after three, and it was amazing what a good night of sleep could do. Bess, George, and I had all woken up feeling much better, and from the look of Veronica, who was having her makeup done a few feet away, she was feeling much better too. The sad, hollow look was gone from her eyes, and she looked bright and excited and silly—just like you would expect a bride to feel on her wedding day.

And it *was* her wedding day, officially—Xavier had texted all the guests after he'd returned from the hospital the night before with his arm in a cast and all his bumps and bruises bandaged up. He would have to forgo the planned BASE jump (though Veronica, apparently, was still planning to do it), but the wedding was *on*.

George, who, like me, was already dressed and made-up, lifted a finger to her matte red lips and glanced at me like, *Want to handle this one, Nancy?* George was wearing her usual classic black sheath dress with a chic twist effect at the neckline, but she claimed she wasn't *into* fashion or hairstyling.

"I *like* it," I insisted, gesturing to Bess's updo with my right hand. "Is it retro? Sure. But that's what makes it unexpected and fun."

Bess ran a hand over the blond hair at her crown, which had been twisted into a sort of pompadour, leading back into a complicated knot. "*Chic* unexpected and fun?" she asked.

"Absolutely," Veronica chimed in. "You should ask how she did that look! You could wear it to dances and stuff!"

Finally Bess broke into a relieved smile. "It *is* cute, huh?" she asked, smoothing down her red satin brides-maid dress. Veronica had let each woman in her wedding party choose their own dress style in the same fabric, and Bess had chosen a cute slip-dress style with twisted straps and an A-line skirt. It suited her perfectly.

"You look like a million dollars, Bess," I said, then gestured around the room. "You *all* do."

Deanna, who was ready to go and sitting on the bed, grinned at me and flipped her red satin cape-let behind her shoulders. "Thanks, Nancy. You and George look super cute too. Don't let the kids get their sticky fingers all over you!"

"They won't have a chance," George replied. "We've got plenty of games and toys to keep them busy. There *may* even be a screening of *Toy Story* on my iPad."

Deanna grinned. "Omigosh, you've figured them out."

George nodded. "When in doubt, Pixar. That's the main lesson I've learned in all my babysitting days."

As Deanna and George continued to chitchat, I looked over at Priya. She was sitting in an armchair near the window, looking out at the Strip with a tense expression. As I watched, she turned around, then slowly stood and walked over to stand behind Veronica.

The hairstylist was just pinning one last curled lock into place. She held up her hands and stood back, meeting Veronica's eyes in the mirror. "There you are, gorgeous. Anything you'd like to change?"

Veronica stared at herself in the mirror. For a moment she just looked stunned, like she couldn't believe her reflection was real. There was something in her eyes that I couldn't quite read—nerves?

She cleared her throat. "I wish our parents were here," she said, glancing at Deanna.

Oh, of course. I felt like a blockhead. It was only natural for Veronica to look a little sad—she was getting married without her parents in attendance.

Deanna stood. "Me too, *hermana*. But you know how much I love and support you. They'll come around."

"Ready for this?" The hairstylist lifted a crystal headpiece from the counter. Since veils and roller coasters don't mix, Veronica had explained, she would attach the veil to this headpiece after the ride was over.

She nodded now. "Yes, please."

We all watched as the hairstylist pinned the headpiece in place on the side of Veronica's head. Long, dark waves cascaded from it, down Veronica's back. She looked gorgeous. She looked like a bride.

She stared at her reflection. Her eyes were wide, and was that a tear in the corner of the left one? It would be natural for a bride to feel emotional on her wedding day, I reminded myself. But I remembered how hollow she'd seemed on the observation deck the night before. All morning, she'd been the cheerful Veronica I'd known since she'd become engaged to Xavier—but now, suddenly, she was *that* Veronica again. The Veronica who'd sadly gazed down at the Strip, who hadn't stayed with her fiancé at the hospital.

Priya cleared her throat, watching her friend in the mirror. "Ronny," she said softly. "I just want . . . I mean, are you sure about this?"

Veronica met her eyes in the mirror. "I'm sure," she said tightly. *I don't want to talk about it*, her tone made clear.

Priya shook her head. She seemed to be struggling to find the right words. "I know you love him," she said in a low voice. "But your parents aren't even here, and maybe their concerns about him make sense? I just want you to be safe."

Veronica watched Priya's reflection. "Priya, I love you. But you don't have to worry about me. I know how to keep myself safe," she said simply.

Priya stared at her for a second longer, then nodded and backed away.

"So," Deanna said, shooting an annoyed glance at Priya before turning back to her sister, "are you ready to get married, sis?"

Veronica stared at her reflection for a moment longer, then took a deep breath and stood.

"Let's do this!" she shouted.

"I broke my purple crayon," Lakshmi whined an hour or so later. She lifted a brand-new Crayola, broken in half.

"No worries," George said, swiftly pulling the crayon from her grasp. "That's why we sprang for the box of one hundred twenty, kiddo. I bet we can find you another purple in here that's just as good."

I glanced over at the entrance to the Skytop Screamer roller coaster, a ride that was mostly unremarkable except for *where* its track was located: at the tippy top of the Soar skyscraper. Riders got strapped in to wind around the outside of the observation deck—even, for one brief but pants-wetting moment, dangling upside down over the edge of the building. This coaster was *not for* me—not even for extreme-sports-curious, open-minded Nancy Drew—but it was definitely for people like Xavier and Veronica, which was why they were kicking off their wedding ceremony with a joint ride on the Screamer.

Xavier waited at the ride entrance, along with Max, who would be officiating the ceremony. They both looked very smart in coordinated gray tuxedos. Four rows of guests in folding chairs were seated nearby, including the wedding party. I caught Arlo's eye and he nodded at me and smiled. George and I had been placed at a picnic table where we could mind the kiddos, but our table had a great view of the action. And so far the kids, who were adorable in their wedding finery, had been very well-behaved. We hadn't even had to break out *Toy Story* or the emergency snacks.

"Always and Forever" suddenly started blaring on the outdoor speakers, and the sliding doors to the elevators opened, revealing Veronica. She beamed at Xavier, and any sadness or hesitation I'd seen in her suite was totally gone. She wore the look of a bride who was marrying someone she truly loved. Xavier beamed right back at her, and George nudged me with her elbow. When I turned to look at her, her eyes were teary.

"Weddings," she said, shaking her head. "They get me every time."

"George!" I whispered fiercely. "I had no idea. You're such a softie!"

"Don't tell Bess," she whispered back. "I need to preserve my reputation as the strong cousin."

Veronica walked up to Xavier, who whispered something to her and took her hand.

"Ladies and gentlemen," Max announced into a wireless microphone, "and guests following on social media, before the ceremony, as part of their walk down the aisle, Veronica and Xavier would like to celebrate their love with a ride on the Skytop Screamer."

He walked up the few stairs to the platform where riders boarded and attached something to the hood of the front car.

"What's that?" I whispered to George.

"I think it's some kind of camera," she whispered back. "For the livestream."

After Max descended, Xavier led Veronica up the stairs and helped a young woman in a Soar uniform strap Veronica into the front car. Then Xavier got in next to her, and the young woman strapped him in and then pulled down a restraining bar.

"Here we go," Max announced as the woman took a step away and pressed a huge red button on a support beam.

"Aaaagghhhh!" Veronica started screaming immediately as the cars rocketed into motion. We watched as the coaster rapidly snaked around the edges of the observation deck, then descended out of sight, down around the sides of the casino building. Xavier and Veronica both screamed when, I assumed, the car flipped upside down, and then there was more screaming and laughter until, only a couple of minutes after departing, the coaster zoomed back to the platform.

Max climbed the stairs and held up the microphone. "How was it?" he asked the couple as the Soar employee returned to raise the restraining bar and help them out of their seats.

Veronica couldn't seem to stop laughing.

"It was amazing!" Xavier replied, grabbing the mic. "The best coaster I've ever been on! Dude, when I was hanging upside down over the Strip there, just staring down at all the people and feeling my heart pound through my chest, all I could think was, *'Man! I'm so happy I'm doing this with Veronica!'* And after today, we'll never be apart, baby!"

He leaned over to kiss her, and when he pulled away, I could see that Veronica was holding the crystal headpiece on with her right hand.

"That was fantastic," she agreed. "And I can't wait to make this official, baby! But I think I'm having a wardrobe malfunction. Can you all give me a sec to get this thing pinned back on?"

Xavier said of course, and Veronica jumped up and carefully descended the stairs, holding the headpiece the whole time. With her left hand, she gave an awkward wave to the assembled guests. "Be right back!" she promised.

Deanna moved toward her, now holding the

pristine white veil she'd retrieved from a bag near the altar. "Can I help?" she asked. "You know I'm a ninja with a bobby pin!"

Veronica turned around, caught her sister's eye, and chuckled. "No need, sis," she insisted. "I've got this. Just give me a minute." She disappeared through the sliding doors.

"Nancy!" Deanna's older son, Luka, suddenly tugged on my wrap. "Do you know how to play tic-tac-toe?"

So soon Luka and I were engaged in a very serious tic-tac-toe battle. When he finally tired of it and turned his attention to a sticker book, I shot a curious look at George. "How long has she been gone?" I asked. The guests looked like they were starting to get restless, a few standing up, stretching, or walking around the roof-deck. Xavier, who had been chatting amiably with the guests at first, was beginning to look more tense, his eyes repeatedly returning to the sliding doors.

George tapped her watch. "About fifteen minutes?" she guessed.

I looked at her, and I could tell by her awkward expression that we were both wondering the same thing. *How long does it take to pin a headpiece back on?*

After a few more minutes went by, I whispered to George, "The hairstylist took maybe two or three minutes to get it on in the first place, right?"

George shrugged. "Maybe the elevator got stuck?" she suggested. "Maybe Veronica spilled something on herself or had some kind of pre-wedding calamity? Oh, look."

She pointed toward the roller-coaster platform. Xavier, who was fully frowning by now, had gestured for Bess, Deanna, and Priya to come over to him, and was whispering to them animatedly. When he was finished, the women nodded and headed toward the door to the elevators.

George shot me a look, and I knew instantly to jump up and follow them. "I can handle the kiddos for a few minutes," she promised.

"What's going on?" I asked Bess as I rushed inside just as the elevator arrived with a ding.

Bess and Priya both wore tense faces. Deanna looked a little more relaxed.

"Xavier just wants us to go check on Veronica," Bess explained. "You know, it's been awhile."

"Is it okay if I come along?" I asked.

"Sure," Priya replied, at the same time Deanna said, "I guess so." As we all piled into the elevator, Deanna shook her head.

"I'm sure she's fine," she said, pressing the button for forty-four, Veronica's floor. "She's not like a makeup and hair girl. She's probably just having trouble getting the headpiece to stay on. I should have come with her in the first place, honestly."

Priya's lips were pursed tight. "I guess we'll see," she said, but she didn't look convinced.

When the elevator stopped on the forty-fourth floor, we all nearly knocked one another over rushing out. We ran down the hall to Veronica's suite. The door was closed.

"Veronica!" Priya yelled, pounding on the door. "It's your bridesmaids! Where are you? Do you need help?"

But there was no answer. No movement inside the room. It sure sounded like no one was in there.

I was beginning to get a weird, panicky tingle under my skin. Suddenly all I could think about was Veronica's red, hollow eyes the night before. *I knew something was off!*

Deanna whipped out a key card.

"Where the heck did you get that?" Bess asked.

"Pockets," Deanna said proudly, wiggling her fingers inside a pocket over her hips. "My dress has them. Don't be jealous."

"I *am*, though," Bess pouted as Deanna stuck the card in the lock. Bess ran her hands over the hips of her dress, where pockets would be.

"Ladies, focus," Priya said sharply as the door clicked open.

The suite was dark. We cautiously stepped in, calling for Veronica, but there was no light in the bedroom or bathroom. In fact, everything looked exactly as we'd left it. Veronica's purse was open on the bed, its contents spilling out from when she'd ransacked it looking for a last-minute breath mint. George had changed her shoes right before we'd left, leaving her tall boots just inside the entryway, blocking the hallway—no one had disturbed them.

And a bride, rushing to fix her hair and get back to the ceremony, likely would have knocked at least one over.

Now I leaned down and pushed them against the wall. Priya was running in and out of all the rooms. "She's not here," she said sharply, looking from Bess to Deanna.

"It looks like she wasn't here at all," I said, gesturing to the purse and the boots.

Deanna frowned. "Probably we crossed each other in the elevators, and she's already back up on the roof-deck," she suggested.

"Or maybe she didn't come down here to fix her hair after all?" Bess hypothesized. She looked nervous, but like she was trying to hold it together. "Maybe she was in a public restroom closer to the roof-deck?"

I let out a tiny sigh. I knew where Deanna and Bess

were coming from, but none of their theories were sooth-ing the tingle under my skin. The suite looked like it hadn't been touched since we'd left. And there wasn't a rest-room on the roof-deck level, which meant that Veronica would have had to ride the elevator down at least to the level of the bar/café we'd visited the night before. At that point, why not just go to her suite where she was comfort-able and had hair spray, a brush, extra hairpins?

Priya didn't look like she was buying it either. "Okay," she said in a tight voice, "let's go *now* and see if she's on the roof-deck, then."

"And I'll get out on the floor below," I offered. "I can check the ladies' room there."

No one said anything else as we hurried out of the suite and back to the elevator. We were silent as we waited the thirty seconds or so for the elevator to arrive, and silent when we climbed inside. Everyone, even Deanna, was now wearing a pinched, uncomfortable expression. It felt like we were all trying to believe that everything would be fine, but it was becoming harder and harder.

Ding! We reached the level with the bar/café,

observation deck, and restrooms. I stepped out and waved back at the others.

"I'll text you if I find her," I promised. "Or . . . Deanna's the only one with pockets, huh. Okay, I'll text someone who definitely has their phone on—George."

Bess nodded. "Thanks, Nancy."

The elevator doors slid closed, and I quickly headed for the restroom. I looked around eagerly, but it was empty except for a young girl and her mother. All the stalls were wide open, and the woman was using a wet paper towel to wipe the young girl's face. She looked up at me with a friendly smile.

"This is a weird question, but did you guys see a bride come in here?" I asked.

The woman raised a curious eyebrow. "Why?" she asked. "Did you lose one?"

I cleared my throat. "Uh, yeah. Yes, actually."

The little girl giggled, and the woman shook her head. "I had terrible jitters the morning before my wedding," she said. "Maybe she got cold feet. Just give her some time."

I nodded and thanked them, then quickly checked the bar. Nothing. As I was walking back to the elevator, my eye caught the observation deck, and I felt a chill, remembering how sadly Veronica had been staring out at the Strip the night before. Could she have come back here? Shivering, I ran out there and looked around, peering over the edge of the deck, but there was nothing out of the ordinary. No sign that Veronica had been here at all.

So where *was* she?

As I got back into the elevator, I pictured Veronica's face as she'd walked out onto the roof-deck and caught Xavier's eye. That was real love in her eyes, I was sure of it. And she'd been laughing and smiling on the roller coaster. She was happy to be marrying the man she loved—at least, that was what it looked like.

Why would she run away from her own wedding?

When the elevator doors opened, I could tell immediately from the vibe outside that Veronica wasn't there. Guests were standing in groups, huddling, whispering to one another with concerned looks on their faces.

Xavier and Max were having an intense conversation by the roller coaster entrance, neither looking happy.

All eyes turned to me when I walked through the sliding door. Without a word, I shook my head.

"Noooooo!" Xavier let out a wail, and Max walked over to one of the guests, who, I now realized, was holding up an iPhone on a selfie stick, likely livestreaming the whole wedding. He started to gesture for him to turn it off, but Xavier ran over, again shouting, "No!"

Xavier pointed at the lens of the camera. "I want them to see! I want all my fans to help me! Listen, something happened to Veronica! If any of you are in the Las Vegas area, I need you to get out there and look for her! She was last seen—"

"Wait, wait!" George had stood up from the kiddie table and walked to Xavier. I glanced over and saw Priya holding Lakshmi in her lap, and Deanna whispering to Luka and Miranda.

Xavier looked at George, annoyed. "What?"

George frowned at him, then looked at the guest. "Turn it off, please."

"What?!" Xavier looked from Max to George, wearing the expression of a teenage boy who's just been told to power down his gaming system. "*Why?* My followers are my fam, bro! There's nothing you can say to me that you can't say in front of them. . . ."

He trailed off as the guest who was filming pressed something and nodded at George. "It's off," he said.

Xavier let out a moan. George reached out and put a hand on his shoulder. "I know this is hard," she said. "I know it's not what you expected. But you have to consider the possibility that she just didn't *want* to marry you."

Xavier let out an anguished sound, and Bess, who had been cautiously approaching, shot her cousin a reproachful look. "Way harsh, George!"

George held up her hand. "I know, I know! But she's a grown woman, and she might have her reasons for leaving! We can't send hundreds of strangers after Veronica in a city she doesn't know. There are other ways to get to the bottom of this."

Xavier groaned. "How? I *know* something happened

to her. I know that girl! Veronica loves me! You can't fake that!"

George caught my eye. "Well . . . let me present my friend." She gestured toward me dramatically, like on a game show when the spokesmodel shows off a *brand-new car!* "Nancy isn't just Bess's and my BFF for, like, ever. She's also a kick-butt detective. And finding people is kind of her thing."

CHAPTER SIX

There Goes the Bride

THERE WAS NO TIME TO LOSE. ONCE XAVIER reluctantly agreed that, yes, I could start a search for Veronica and we could keep the cameras off until I got a better idea of what had happened to her, I hustled back into the elevator and headed down. This time, I went straight to the casino floor.

"Where are we going? Are we even allowed to be here?" asked Bess, who had followed me along with George. "Aren't we underage?"

I could barely hear her with all the binging and bonging and clanking change sounds, not to mention the music that was pumping in at what had to be an unhealthy volume. Bright lights shone all over the casino floor, making it look like daylight at any hour. "I'm pretty sure you're right," I admitted. "But just . . . wait."

I hadn't spent a lot of time in casinos. But I had watched enough casino heist movies to know that casinos had *massive* security centers . . . security centers that they are notoriously secretive about, because people tend to stop having fun and spending money when they realize their every move is being tracked. I needed to get inside somehow. But I had a feeling that a teenage girl just showing up at the hotel's front desk and asking for an invitation wouldn't be taken very seriously.

I walked over to a slot machine, looked around, and perched on the seat in front of it. Looking at the screen, I could barely make sense of it. The machine was branded with a network TV game show host, whose voice enticed me to "spin the wheel!" But the game was video-based, meaning there was nothing *really* spinning. Tiny icons formed five rows and three columns. Lines framed the screen, showing all the different sets of images you could use to win—*if* you paid enough money.

"Nancy!" George hissed. "I don't know what's gotten into you, but for heaven's sake, slots have the *worst* odds of any game in here! It's simple math! Not to mention, they're all—"

"Excuse me, miss?" A stocky, friendly looking man, dressed in black pants and a black satin jacket, had sidled up to me while George was giving her rant. "Can I see some ID, please?"

I turned to him. "Are you security?"

He nodded and tapped his name tag, which was made to look like a police badge. It read PARKER. I wasn't sure whether that was his first or last name. "If you can't produce an ID, I'm afraid you'll need to come with me."

"To the security office?" I asked eagerly.

He looked nonplussed. "No," he said. "But I suspect you're underage, and I need you to leave the gaming floor."

I reached into my tiny purse and pulled out my driver's license. "I *am* underage. And I sat at this slot machine. Now don't you need to take me to the security office?"

Parker had gone from nonplussed to confused. "Miss, are you well? It's not against the law to sit at a slot machine. But as you are underage, I will escort you off the gaming floor."

"I'm underage too," George blurted, producing her own driver's license.

"Me too," Bess added, "but I don't have ID because I didn't get the dress with pockets."

Parker's polished demeanor was cracking. He furrowed his brows, looking from Bess, to George, to me.

"The thing is," I said, "we all probably *should* go to the security office, because we're having an emergency."

It makes sense for casinos to be serious about security. After all, they don't just need to protect their employees and patrons from crime being committed inside the casino; they also need to make sure that no one is cheating the casino. And because that's a multimillion-dollar proposition, there is basically no spot in a casino or related property that isn't watched over by one or more security cameras.

I explained what had happened at the wedding to Parker as he very reluctantly led us out a nondescript doorway hidden behind a bank of poker machines, down a brightly lit hallway, and to a heavy reinforced steel door that was, almost definitely, locked.

"That sounds terrible," Parker said, "and I understand why you're concerned, but I'm telling you, *no civilian* gets inside the Soar security office."

"But Parker, weren't you listening?" I asked. "She left her purse and wallet behind! Doesn't that sound suspicious to you? If one of your security cameras got footage of where Veronica went, it could help us understand whether she disappeared on her own—or was *taken* by somebody."

Parker made a low sound in his throat—annoyance he was trying to tamp down, I suspected—and shook his head. "A runaway bride," he said, "is not a crime. I suggest you go to the police and engage their help. If they decide a crime has been committed on Soar property, they can demand our footage, and we will hand it over."

I sighed.

"The groom is already alerting the police," Bess said. "In fact, he was on the phone on the roof-deck when we left him. But surely you know that when a person goes missing, the first twenty-four hours are when they're most likely to be found alive? Time is of the *essence* here, sir!"

Parker frowned at Bess, then at me. "No one gets behind that door unless you work here," he insisted.

George had pulled out her phone and was fussing with it. Without another word, she suddenly pushed the screen toward Parker. I heard Xavier's anguished cry from when I'd stepped onto the roof-deck a few minutes earlier.

As Xavier began ranting into the camera, Parker turned to me. "What is this?"

"It's a livestream," I replied without missing a beat. "It's already gone out to Redd Zone's two hundred fifty thousand followers. And it's pretty intense, so it's likely to go viral." I paused, and George stopped the video.

"Unless I'm mistaken," I went on, "that video sure makes it look like a bride was kidnapped or worse in this very casino. Once that gets out, I suspect people are going to think twice about getting married here. Or staying in the hotel. Or spending their money in the casino. It could be devastating for the Soar, which is such a shame! It's such a high-end place, which someone clearly spent a lot of money to build and maintain. If only some smart, enterprising, underage girl could prove once and for all that nothing nefarious happened to this woman at the Soar . . ."

Parker scowled, then ran his hand over his face. He pulled a card from a lanyard around his neck and pressed it to a reader on the reinforced door, which opened with a snick.

"Let's make this quick," he said. "The boss is not going to be happy."

He opened the door and stepped inside. We followed him. Almost immediately, I gasped. I'd been expecting a bunch of people watching security cameras, but nothing could have prepared me for how *vast* the dimly lit space was, and how many people there were, watching a seemingly endless number of cameras. As soon as the door opened to reveal us, it was like time stopped. Everyone turned from the screens they were monitoring to stare at three teenage guests in semiformal attire—guests who *definitely* didn't belong.

"Who in the name of all that's holy is *that*?" an irritated female voice demanded from the darkness.

Parker cleared his throat. "This here is Nancy Drew," he said, "and I can explain."

After much deliberation and explaining, the three of us were put in a private room and given a laptop loaded with the afternoon's footage from the roof-deck; the elevators; the floor where the observation deck, restrooms, and bar/café were; and Veronica's floor.

"There she is," Bess said right away as, onscreen,

Veronica entered the elevator from the roof-deck in her wedding dress, still holding the crystal head-piece.

We all watched, transfixed, as she pressed a button and got off on the floor below.

"The observation deck floor!" I cried. "So she *did* go down to use the restroom there."

There were no security cameras in the restrooms, obviously (gross). But when we switched to the footage from the floor with the bar/café, we saw Veronica enter the restroom . . . and then nothing.

Ten minutes went by. Fifteen. "I don't get it, guys," I complained. "I looked in there! She was not in the restroom when I got there. And the mother and daughter who *were* in there hadn't seen her."

"But we don't see her come out," Bess said, biting her lip.

"Or *do* we?" George asked. "We do see a few people go in and out after Veronica goes in. Are we sure one of them isn't . . . ?"

I hit rewind. We went back to when Veronica

disappeared into the restroom. An older woman wearing a velour lounge suit exited the restroom, futzing with her curls. Then two young women in braids and matching family reunion T-shirts, laughing hysterically as they headed to the bar/café. And then . . .

"There!" Bess cried. The timestamp on the video put it just three minutes after Veronica had entered. "Check her out."

It was another older woman, or so I'd thought, dressed in a baggy sweatshirt over a turtleneck, thick leggings, and a baseball cap that said WHAT HAPPENS IN VEGAS . . .

"But her hair!" I cried. "It looks short and gray."

"No, look at that walk," George said, pointing. "I know my cousin. Bess is right: that's Veronica."

We were all silent for a moment as we digested that fact—and what it meant.

"She stashed clothes in the restroom," I said, struggling to believe it.

"She stashed *a wig* in the restroom," George added.

Bess shook her head. "She planned this," she said.

"I don't know why, but Veronica planned to leave Xavier at the altar—and disappear."

I thought back again to when we'd seen Veronica the night before on the observation deck. The red eyes, the sadness in her gaze—was it related to this, knowing she planned to leave? Then I thought of how Veronica had beamed when the door to the roof-deck opened and she first saw Xavier. *She loved him.* At least, in the moment, I had been sure of it. And that certainly matched how she'd acted every time I'd seen the couple together before that point, since they'd gotten engaged.

Why, then? Why had she become a runaway bride?

We went back to the elevator footage and found Veronica—in her old-woman disguise—getting back in and riding the elevator to the third floor, the floor that housed the casino's buffet and pricey steakhouse. We could see the door open, and Veronica talking to someone outside the elevator. After a moment, she exited. We waited for a few minutes, but she never got back into the elevator.

"We need more footage," Bess said with a sigh.

When we went back out into the security office to request footage from the third floor, we learned that security guards had searched all public areas of the casino but had found no sign of Veronica. I told them about the disguise, but they said they had seen no trace of the disguised Veronica either. Deanna had allowed them into her suite and they saw the same things we had—her purse, including her phone, left on the bed. No indication that she had been back after we left to go to the wedding.

Now the security head, the woman who'd demanded to know who we were when Parker brought us into the office, came with us into the little room where we sat down to view the third-floor footage. Her name tag read FLORA.

"I have to hand it to you kids," she said, reaching for the mouse that sped up or slowed down footage. "You've figured out more in a couple of hours than I've seen detectives put together in days."

"Whoa," George breathed when the third-floor

footage came up onscreen. "This isn't going to be easy."

The hallway that the elevators exited onto on the third floor was mobbed. "The third floor is where the buffet is," Flora explained. "It's kind of a big deal in Vegas. And this was right around the early bird specials."

We watched the same five minutes over and over, but while we could sort of see someone who looked like Veronica in disguise exit the elevator, the crowd seemed to absorb her completely. When the crowd had moved on, she was gone. There was no telling what had happened to her.

Flora demanded footage of all the stairways and exits from the third floor, and it took at least an hour to carefully watch it all, but there was no sign of Veronica leaving the building.

Bess coughed. "So she's still—*here*?" she asked incredulously. "In the casino, in disguise or something?"

Flora huffed. "If you were a runaway bride, and you took time to put together this disguise and plan your exit this carefully . . . would *you* stay in the same casino as all your guests and your former fiancé?"

George shook her head. "Definitely not. But there's no footage of her leaving. . . ."

"Well." Flora shook her head. "Here's the thing, girls. And I can tell you this because you're underage, and if I catch you out on the gaming floor, I'll have you arrested. Our security system is pretty tight, but there are holes—every system has holes. Cameras get damaged and need repair, and there are spots in the stairwells the cameras don't catch. Ways to sneak out in a crowd and not be detected. If your friend knew what she was doing, she could most certainly have gotten out."

I looked at my friends. George looked thoughtful, and Bess's eyes were wide.

"And she could be anywhere by now," I filled in. "Anywhere at all."

The security team searched the restaurant floor but found no further sign of Veronica.

"What about the police?" Bess asked as we left, blinking helplessly as we stepped from the dark security office into the bright white hallway. "Xavier was going to call them."

"And he did," Flora replied. "We've been cooperating with them. They're questioning Xavier. Dude doesn't seem to know much, but when a bride runs like this, you have to wonder what she's running from. I'm sorry, girls—I think we've done all we can for today."

I swallowed hard as we left Flora and the security office behind. I couldn't help thinking of Priya's face when she'd told Veronica in the suite earlier that she didn't have to marry Xavier. She didn't trust him, and neither did Veronica's parents. Arlo had said he couldn't count on Xavier. Veronica had left him at the hospital the night before.

But they loved each other. I had been so sure when they saw each other on the roof-deck.

Maybe, in this case, love just wasn't enough to go through with the wedding?

My friends and I quickly moved past the gaming

floor and took the elevator to the buffet. It was eight thirty at night, later than it felt like it should be, but the security office and the gaming floor had no windows, and I had always heard that casinos pumped in lots of fresh oxygen to make gamblers feel more awake. I felt disoriented and fairly sick to my stomach, but George insisted that we should sit down and eat something, or we'd regret it later. So we picked up plates at the end of the buffet bar and began loading up. I could see why Flora had said it was kind of a big deal in Vegas—all you could eat for just $12.99! And there were high-end items on the buffet, like shrimp and prime rib. I almost wished I was hungrier.

I lingered at the salad bar, trying to pick things that looked fresh and easy on the stomach. When I got back to the table, George and Bess were staring at George's phone in a way that made me think a Significant Development had occurred. "What's up?" I asked.

George turned the phone to face me. "Xavier is out of questioning," she said. "He texted us to see what we learned. Should we cooperate with him?"

Bess cleared her throat. "It *does* seem like Veronica left on purpose, with the disguise and everything. It makes me wonder if we can trust him."

I nodded. "I get that," I said, "but he's going to find out what we know eventually anyway, if the security here is cooperating with the police. We might as well learn what *he* knows. Want to invite him down here to debrief?"

George nodded and began typing on her phone. I took a few half-hearted bites of my meal, and the food was making me feel a little better. A few minutes later, Xavier arrived. He was wearing sweatpants and a Redd Zone hoodie, and he looked, if this was possible in the scant hours since we'd seen him on the roof-deck, like he'd been awake for seventy-two hours straight. His eyes were red and a little swollen, implying tears. But he looked relieved to see us as he sat down at our table.

"What happened?" Bess asked him. "You go first."

Xavier sighed. "They questioned me for hours, bro. But in the end, they said they didn't have a reason to suspect me." He went on to say that he'd told the cops that his and Veronica's relationship had never been better. After a while, the police explained to him that security footage showed Veronica changing into a disguise and leaving, and that the disguise implied that she left of her own free will. They thought she probably got cold feet.

"But I just know that's not it," Xavier said, pressing his fingers to his temples. "V is my soulmate. I would know if she wanted to leave me. Something happened. And I'm afraid someone did something to her."

George looked sympathetic, but she still pressed. "But how do you explain the disguise, then? She had to have planted that earlier."

Xavier winced and nodded. "I know. I know. Maybe someone threatened her if she went through with the wedding. Maybe she had something going on that she wanted to work out on her own before we got married. I don't know! All I know is, V loved me too much to leave me like this. There's something bigger going on—something we're not seeing yet."

I caught Bess's eye, and I could tell that she, too,

was struggling with Xavier's explanation. The *easiest* answer was certainly that Veronica had chosen to leave. But at the same time, something about his manner made me believe Xavier. I knew not everyone trusted him, but it felt to me like he was telling the truth.

Still—that didn't mean Xavier knew everything about his bride-to-be, or what she really felt about him.

"So the police aren't doing anything?" I asked after a moment.

"Well, they're filing a missing person report," Xavier replied. "Her leaving behind her wallet and cell phone was enough evidence of that. They've put out a trace on her credit cards. But they say there's not much else they can do, unless I find evidence of a crime. Until then, I don't think this is high priority for them."

There was a moment of sad silence, none of us knowing quite what to say. We filled Xavier in on what we'd learned in the security office, but he knew most of it already from the police. When we finished our meal, it seemed like there wasn't much left to do but turn in for the night.

Xavier looked teary again. "I just know she wouldn't leave me," he whimpered. "She'd never make me feel like this on purpose. She's the love of my life! Something *happened* to her, I know it."

As Bess and George leaned in to comfort him, I had a sudden brain wave. "If there's no crime, according to the police, does that mean they didn't take evidence?" I asked. "Meaning you still have her phone?"

Xavier looked a little startled, but then nodded. "Yeah, I have it."

"Do you know the passcode?" I asked. "Do you mind if I do a little poking around in it, looking for clues?"

I stared into Xavier's eyes. See, this is a big test for possible criminals: a guilty person will *not* want to hand over evidence that might get them caught. But Xavier looked totally open, maybe even relieved. "That would be amazing, Nancy," he said, seemingly earnestly. "I'll give it to you, and the passcode is 10-23. That's the day we met."

He smiled a little sadly. We packed up our things

and followed Xavier back to his room, where we waited in the hall while he got Veronica's phone and handed it to me.

"Listen, tell me anything you find out, if it might mean she's safe." He hesitated. "Even—even if you think it's something I might not want to know. Even if she doesn't want to marry me, I just want to know she's okay."

I nodded. "I'll definitely do that, Xavier. Now, try to get some sleep."

We said our goodbyes. Exhausted, Bess, George, and I summoned the elevator to go down to our floor. But when the elevator doors opened, they revealed a familiar face.

"Priya!" Bess said. "How are you doing?"

As we crowded in, I noticed that Priya was still wearing her red satin bridesmaid dress, but her hair had fallen a bit and she looked worn out. She was leaning precariously against the railing on the back wall.

"I'm *fiiiine*," Priya replied, shifting to lean against the corner. "And you? What've you all been doing since the . . . the *wedding that wassssshn't*?" She laughed at her own joke, a little too hard.

I exchanged glances with Bess and George. It looked like Priya had spent a lot of the hours since Veronica disappeared at the bar. Her slurred speech and awkward balance told me she had been drinking.

"We've been trying to figure out what happened to Veronica," I said. "You know, talking to security and stuff."

Priya's eyes widened. "Oh, why would you do that? There'sh no need."

Bess frowned. "What do you mean there's no need?"

"Issshhhn't it obviousss?" Priya asked. "Veronica finally *lissshened* to me and got shmart. She ran away."

"From what?" Bess asked. The elevator dinged to a stop: fourteenth floor. It wasn't where we were staying, so it had to be Priya's floor.

"From Xavier," Priya said, lunging toward the open door. "She finally saw it. That guy was going to *kill* her."

CHAPTER SEVEN

~

Insomniac Investigations

"WHAT DOES THAT MEAN?" I BLURTED, throwing out my arm to stop the elevator from closing. "You can't just drop an accusation like that and then leave!"

Priya turned around to face me, half-in, half-out of the elevator. Her eyes were a little unfocused. "What do you mean, '*drop*'?" she asked. "I've been sshaying this from the beginning. All those exshtreme sports! Veronica was never into that before. She's just lucky it was *him* that crashed into that tree. If it was her, I'm not sure she would have survived."

"Ohhhhhh," Bess breathed, sounding very relieved. "You mean that the sports he got her into were dangerous, then? Not that he was literally going to murder her?"

Priya scrunched up her eyebrows, looking almost annoyed. "Of course not! Sheesh. But he's still bad news, and she finally figured it out. The *real* Veronica ishn't about that life."

I sighed and pulled my arm back, letting Priya exit. "Okay, okay. Point taken. Good night, Priya. Get some rest." *And sleep it off,* I added silently. As Veronica's best friend headed off and the door closed behind her, I wondered about her words. Veronica *had* run away from the wedding on purpose; the disguise proved that. So was there any truth to what Priya believed? Had Veronica tired of Xavier's thrill seeking, maybe gotten scared straight by his accident at the rehearsal dinner? Was it as simple as that?

Bess, George, and I stumbled back to our room and quickly got ready for bed. Soon after we turned out the lights, I could hear their breathing slowing enough to imply that they'd both fallen asleep. Bess muttered a couple of incomprehensible things in her sleep, like she does. But I felt as wide awake as if I'd just pulled the curtain to reveal a blinding-white morning and drunk three espressos. I felt a little jealous of my friends, that they were able to press pause on a mystery and relax enough to go to sleep. I wasn't so good at that.

Fortunately, I had something to keep me occupied. After a few minutes of tossing and turning, I threw off the covers, got up, and fished Veronica's phone out of my purse. I typed 1023 on the keypad, and sure enough, the phone unlocked. *Well, that's a note in Xavier's favor,* I thought, clicking on the messages icon. If Xavier thought that Veronica had reason to fear him, he wouldn't be so eager to share her phone with me . . . would he?

Or was there a chance he was playing me? Could he have deleted anything compromising before he gave me the phone? But he hadn't had that kind of time, had he? And how could he have known I would ask for it?

I shook my head. I was spiraling. *Just look at the phone, Nance,* I reminded myself.

Right. Phone. Clues!

The first conversation in the messages app was between Veronica and Xavier, which made sense. As a loving couple about to get married, they were probably in the closest contact of *anyone* Veronica knew. My pulse quickening, I rapidly scanned through pages and pages of messages, looking for a fight, a harsh word, any indication that not all was well in paradise. But what I found was . . . well, not at all harsh. In fact, it was all pretty squishy. From the morning of the wedding:

Woke up smiling and thinking of you, mariposa.

Awww, babe. You are the sweetest!

I can't wait to call you my wife. Are you nervous?

About screwing up my vows? Sure. :) But I love you so much, babe. I know you'll keep me safe. Won't you?

Forever and ever. <3 <3 <3

It was hard not to gag on all the sweetness. *Gosh*, I wondered, *should I be talking to Ned like that?* I'd texted him once since we'd arrived in Vegas, sending him a video George took of me flyboarding with the message, *Did you see this one coming?* He'd texted back, *You're a woman of constant surprises, Nancy*, and then the heart emoji.

Texts between Xavier and Veronica going back over the last few days looked like more of the same. No indication that she was scared—of him, or of anything else. She seemed to be really having a good time in Vegas and looking forward to the wedding. But then why had she decided to run?

Runaway brides don't just happen. There has to be a reason. . . .

I clicked on the next conversation. The first text, the one on the preview page, was from Priya:

I just don't want you to look back on this as the biggest mistake you ever made.

Well! That seemed a lot more contentious than the Xavier convo. I glanced down, reading a conversation that had started the night before, after Xavier's accident.

He'll be fine. It's all fine, Priya.

It's NOT fine! I know you. You have to be freaking out inside.

I'm fine.

How can you do this for the rest of your life? How many trips to the hospital will you take? How many times will you have to wonder if he'll make it through?

It's who he is, and I love him. It's worth it to me.

Will it be worth it if the next time, it's you on a stretcher?

Veronica!

Are you mad? I don't want to upset you the night before your wedding.

V?

I love you. You know that.

I just don't want you to look back on this as the biggest mistake you ever made.

That was the last text between Priya and Veronica. And the fact that Veronica had stopped responding made me curious. Had Priya's warnings gotten through? Was Priya right that Veronica had run away for fear that Xavier's thrill seeking could kill her? Or was Veronica just tired of having this same conversation with her BFF?

I kept looking through the phone. I was hoping to find texts between Veronica and her parents, but she seemed to have her phone set to delete texts after two weeks, and she hadn't interacted with them in that time. That seemed notable in itself, of course—were her parents so against Xavier that they hadn't even sent a last-minute *congratulations* text? All the messages I did find seemed like such normal, everyday, dentist-appointment-canceling, I'm-going-to-be-five-minutes-late-today-warning, thank-you-for-the-flowers-grandma stuff that I almost felt guilty looking through it all. On her phone, Veronica seemed like exactly who she said she was: a bright young woman who loved her friends and her fiancé and was excited about her wedding. There were no dark secrets, no unexpected grudges.

So then where *was* she? Why had she run?

I was about to give up when I noticed a number with a Chicago area code. It wasn't associated with a contact, meaning this wasn't someone Veronica texted with often. I'd overlooked this one because many of the unidentified numbers were spam, doctors' offices, or charities looking for donations. But when I opened up the conversation, this one looked a little different.

Did u get the documents I sent u?

I did. I don't know what to say.

My heart started to beat a little faster. *I don't know what to say?* It wasn't exactly *Let me tell you why I can't marry Xavier*, but it was the most unexpected thing I'd seen on Veronica's phone. Unfortunately, the conversation ended there. I had no idea who the sender was, or what had shaken Veronica about the documents. It could be her accountant sending her an unexpected tax bill, or something equally unexciting. But this at least gave me something to look for. *Documents!*

The text had been sent the day before—a few hours prior to the rehearsal dinner. That gave me a window. I pulled up Veronica's email app. It connected to two accounts—her work account and her personal email. I scrolled down through the list of messages, looking for the little paper clip icon that denotes an attachment. There were two—both work-related things that had nothing to do with the wedding. And based on the messages that accompanied them, neither seemed to be from the mystery texter. They were just documents from colleagues looking to "keep Veronica in the loop."

Figuring that the documents might have been sent a while before the person sent the text, I looked back, one week, two weeks. There were more work-related documents—they took some time to look through, but none seemed pertinent here. Then I checked Veronica's personal email but found only one attachment sent to that account. When I opened it up, I saw an invitation to a friend's baby shower. Could those be the "documents" the texter was asking about? *I don't know what to say.* Maybe Veronica was somehow offended that the person had invited her, or was surprised she was having a baby?

No. Well, maybe, but it seemed extremely unlikely. Who would call a baby shower invite "documents"? And why would Veronica react like that?

No, I told myself, the "documents" had to be something else. My gut told me I hadn't found them yet. I glanced through Veronica's texts, but there were no attachments there, either. Maybe the documents had been sent as a hard copy? If so, my best chance was that they might be in Veronica's room. Maybe she'd brought them with her, or they had been mailed to her at the casino. But I couldn't do anything about that until morning.

Or can I? I had a number. The person who'd sent the text to Veronica didn't *have* to remain a mystery. They were only a phone call away.

I took Veronica's phone into the bathroom and closed the door, not wanting to wake Bess or George. Then I opened the messages icon again and selected the mystery number. I hit the call icon.

As it began to ring, I suddenly felt regretful. It was the middle of the night. *Who wants to get called by a stranger in the middle of the night?* But it was too late to change my mind, because someone was picking up. . . .

"Hello?"

It was a gruff, groggy-sounding male voice. An older man, I guessed from the tone of his voice. And he didn't sound happy.

"Hello, this is a friend of Veronica Vasquez. I think you may have texted her phone earlier?" *What am I saying?* I realized too late that I didn't have a plan. I was just making it up as I went along, which is never good.

The voice turned angry. "Who is this?!"

"This is, ah—like I said. I'm a friend of Veronic—"

"Veronica would never call me in the middle of the night."

Click. The call was ended. I stared at the phone for a second and then, before I could change my mind, I hit *redial. Veronica is missing,* I rehearsed in my mind, *and I wondered from your text if you might have any idea why she disappeared.* I would get it right this time. I would get the—

Bloop. A sad tone sounded from the phone. I pulled it from my ear and read the message:

This call cannot go through because the recipient has blocked your number.

Stupid! I smacked myself on the forehead. *Gah, Nancy, you know better than to just randomly call up people in the middle of the night.* I was tired, wired, and not thinking straight. And I feared I'd just thrown away a potentially helpful source of information.

I sat there for a few minutes, waiting for my breath to go back to normal and thinking through the whole situation. I'd gotten as far as I could tonight. I was tired and making things worse.

I should try to get some rest.

I slunk back into the bedroom and rested Veronica's phone on a desk, far enough from my bed that I'd have to get up to reach it. *That should be enough of a deterrent.*

Then I slid back beneath the covers and tried to take a few deep, soothing breaths.

The curtains were open just a crack, letting in just a tiny bit of the lights of the Strip far below our window. Somewhere out there was Veronica.

If you're out there, I thought, *I hope you're safe. Just hold on.*

I will find you.

CHAPTER EIGHT

~

Rise and Search

I WOKE UP THE NEXT MORNING TO THE smell of bacon. Sunlight was streaming into our room through our partially opened curtains, and when I opened my eyes, I saw Bess and George wheeling a room service cart over to the end of their bed.

"We took the liberty of ordering breakfast, Nancy," Bess said, dramatically lifting off the silver covers of a couple of plates of eggs, potatoes, and bacon as she moved them to a small table. "We figured our brains will need all the fuel they can get today."

I breathed in the sweet, smoky smell and sighed.

"Excellent idea, guys. What time is it? Did I sleep in?"

"Just a little," George replied, pulling up a chair to the food-strewn table. "It's ten thirty. But we figured you needed your sleep."

"Yeah," Bess said, sliding her own chair closer to the table. "*Some* of us might have spotted you playing with that phone late into the night."

I sat up in bed, pushing my hair out of my face. "I thought you two were asleep!"

"We were," Bess said, picking up a slice of bacon and biting it in half. "Mostly. But *this one* has a habit of snoring *and* kicking, and I may have been knocked back into consciousness once or twice. Ow!"

George, now holding her own bacon, smiled sweetly. "Sorry. It's just, I hear I have this habit of kicking."

Bess's eyebrows rose. "Are you denying it? Because I have the bruises on my leg to prove it."

George tilted her head. "You're not such a dream to sleep with yourself, sweetie. I got an earful about . . . well, I'm not sure, honestly. Something to do with Snoopy?"

Bess looked thoughtful. "I think I *did* have a dream where I was in the *Peanuts* Christmas special. We were all singing, you know, that part, '*Loo loo loo loo . . .*'"

I threw off the covers, swung my legs to the floor, then stood up and stretched while Bess and George tried to get to the bottom of who was worse to share a bed with. (From my perspective, it was a tie. And it made me very grateful that I'd won the bed to myself in rock-paper-scissors.)

As I settled in at the table and took the cover off my own plate, George and Bess seemed to declare a cease-fire.

"There *is* an update of sorts," George told me. "I texted Xavier, and there's been no sign of Veronica. No contact with him or anyone he's in contact with."

I sighed. "Well . . . no news is good news, I guess." Although, was that true in a missing person case? Probably not. I poured myself some coffee, thinking that I clearly needed it.

After I'd taken a few bites and a couple of swigs of coffee, it registered that neither of my friends were saying anything. That's unlike them, to say the least. And when I looked up, I could see that they were both staring at me. When I looked from one to the other, Bess turned to George, raising her eyebrows like she was asking George some silent question.

"Is there more?" I asked.

"No. Well, yes. Well, sort of." George put down her fork and leaned forward. "Bess and I were just . . . chatting."

I looked at each of my friends. "Yes?"

"About Veronica," Bess said. "About the possibility that . . . she left on purpose. I mean, we *know* she did, right? She had that disguise ready."

I nodded, shoveling more eggs into my mouth. The disguise was the thing I'd been thinking about the most when it came to this case. Veronica seemed perfectly happy in person and in all her communication. And yet . . . the disguise. *Happy brides-to-be don't plan an escape route.*

"What if she doesn't want to be found, is what we were wondering," George added, a nervous crease appearing in the center of her forehead. "What if Priya was right, and she sensed some danger in Xavier? What if she was doing everything she could to get away for a good reason, and we're just hauling her back?"

I took a sip of coffee and looked at my friends. I could tell from their uncomfortable expressions that this fear was weighing on them.

"That possibility has occurred to me, too," I admitted, putting down my mug. "Veronica is a grown woman, and I would hate to think we might be undoing her escape plan, or putting her back with someone she was afraid of. I get good vibes from Xavier, but she knew him better than any of us, and vibes aren't everything."

Bess nodded. "Exactly. And Veronica isn't exactly the flighty type."

"If she ran," George said, "she must have had a good reason."

"That's sort of why I wanted her phone," I said thoughtfully. "But I've gone through all of it—that *was* what I was doing last night when George was giving you the Rockettes treatment in bed, Bess—and as far as I can tell, it only shows what Xavier has been telling us. They were very much in love, and she was looking forward to getting married."

Bess bit her lip. "Hmm," she said. "I guess that's a relief."

I shrugged. "I guess," I agreed. "But it still leaves a pretty big mystery."

We all ate in silence for a few minutes, thinking our own separate thoughts. When I was beginning to feel more awake, I promised, "Listen, guys. I swear to you, I won't tell Xavier where Veronica is until we know it's safe. But there was one clue on her phone—nothing that implies Xavier was dangerous, *yet*, but I need to check it out. And that means we need to get back into Veronica's room."

"Her room?" Bess perked up. "Sure thing. We can just ask the manager—"

I held up a hand. "Not so fast. We're still checking out Xavier's story, and I can't risk someone at the hotel blurting to him that we asked to be let into her room.

I don't know where Veronica went or who we can trust in the wedding party." I paused. "Which is why we need to break in."

It's nice to have friends who understand you. Who share your inside jokes and funny little shorthand. Who, when you say you have to break into a hotel room, don't say *why* or *how* or *but that's illegal, Nancy.* Instead they just grab a bobby pin from their toiletry bag and stick it into their hair, like George did, and say, "Let's roll."

Bess, George, and I have been around the block together a few times. We've broken into our share of hotel rooms, lockers, and large Swedish furniture stores (that one, only one time). So when we stood outside Veronica's hotel room a few minutes later, it only took George about thirty seconds to use her school ID to disengage the lock.

"There we go," she said as the door snicked open. "Let's see what we can find."

Veronica's suite was still largely as she had left

it. I had explained the documents text to Bess and George, so we all knew what we were looking for. I went for her suitcase first, shoving my hand into the large storage compartments on the inside and outside of the front flap—the perfect place to keep flat documents. But there was nothing inside. I looked around the suitcase a little more, but it was mostly unpacked, so I opened up the closet—hung with clothes, but no signs of paperwork on the shelves. Bess was already searching the desk in the living room, and George was looking through the nightstand. Little by little, we went through all the obvious places you might keep documents, and then ventured to the less obvious places. We pulled all the bedding off the bed and searched it. We looked behind and under all the furniture. I helped Bess pull the mattress off the bed and we looked underneath, then put it back.

Finally, at least an hour later, after we'd searched all the pockets of her remaining clothes, and I had insisted on looking in the toilet tank (nothing) and unscrewing the vent cover from the wall (also nothing), we looked at each other wearily.

"Do we have a plan B?" George asked, trying to brush the dust out of her hair and sneezing loudly.

I sighed. "Not . . . really?" I felt silly admitting it to myself now, but I'd been so sure, so hopeful, that we would find the mysterious documents in Veronica's room, that I hadn't really thought of a plan beyond that. Were we at an impasse?

Bess seemed to read the hopelessness on my face. "Let's sit down and regroup," she suggested, and we all settled next to each other on the now-bare mattress.

I let out a groan. "I just . . . don't know what to do, guys."

Bess's phone suddenly dinged, and she pulled it from her pocket and looked at it in one smooth motion. She looked hopeful at first, but quickly deflated.

"What's that?" George asked.

Bess shook her head. "It's what's-his-name, Xavier's friend from high school."

My ears perked up. "Arlo?" The guy who'd given me such a weird feeling at the rehearsal dinner.

Bess nodded, her lips tight. "He took all our numbers in the wedding party. He was just checking to see if anyone heard anything about Veronica, because his flight leaves tomorrow and he can't afford to change it. Xavier's writing back."

I leaned back on the mattress. "Could *he* be involved?"

George leaned back to look at me. "Arlo? Why?"

I sighed. "I don't know. He seemed awkward and kind of, like, unhappy when I spoke to him at the rehearsal dinner. He said he and Xavier had planned to go into business together, but then he got into some bad stuff and ended up in prison. When he got out, Xavier had already started a business."

Bess pushed her lips to one side, thinking. "You think he's jealous?"

I lifted my hands. "I don't know. But there was that whole thing in his rehearsal-dinner toast about not being able to count on Xavier. Maybe he's still mad and decided to get revenge by doing something to Veronica?"

Bess and George looked thoughtful.

"Except," George said after a few seconds, raising her index finger, "Veronica went willingly, remember? So if anything, he hatched a plan with Veronica to get revenge."

"And her texts just don't imply that," I said, nodding. "I mean, anything's possible. But I would think she would have texted him about it."

We were all quiet for a minute or so. Then, suddenly, Bess jumped up.

"Wait!" she said. "Why aren't we talking about this? Remember in the video, Veronica rode the elevator down to the restaurant level?"

I nodded again, sitting up. "Right, and then she disappeared," I said. "I mean, technically, we don't know she ever left this casino."

Bess held up her hands. "But in the video, on the elevator, she was *talking to somebody*. Remember? When the doors opened?"

I glanced at George, who was glancing at me. We both wore the same expression: *Oh wow. I think she's right.*

"She *could* have been in cahoots with somebody," I said. "Maybe Arlo. But maybe anyone!"

George stood up. "But guys, it was a public elevator. She could have just as easily been giving directions to the buffet to some random stranger, you know?"

I stood up too. "Maybe. And maybe we'll never really be sure. But there's only one way to get an idea of who she might have seen."

We rode the elevator down to the third floor. As soon as the doors opened, we were hit by a cacophony of sounds. Dinging slot machines, raised voices, a hostess yelling for the next party . . . we were facing the casino's enormous, much-advertised buffet. The same place we'd eaten dinner the night before, though I'd barely had an appetite. And then, it hadn't been nearly as busy as it was now. We'd easily gotten a table and been one of maybe six or eight parties inside. Now the dining floor looked packed, and a huge crowd of people waited to be seated—impatiently, based on their facial expressions.

"We put in our name before him," a woman whined to the hostess. The woman looked to be in her seventies, with close-cropped red curls and a sweatshirt embroidered with the Eiffel Tower. "Why are they being seated first?"

The hostess's pleasant expression didn't falter. "He had a party of two, ma'am. You have a party of six."

The woman didn't look convinced. "I don't expect to be here all day. When does the $4.99 lunch special end?"

The hostess glanced at her watch. "Oh, don't worry. It goes until three, and it's barely one."

I slid against the wall, out of the way, and looked back at Bess and George.

"Did she just say $4.99?" Bess asked.

"She did," I replied. "I think that's why it looks like Macy's on Black Friday in here."

George looked at the assembled crowd. "I wouldn't

say Macy's," she said. "I'd say more . . . JCPenney? Sears?"

Bess frowned at her. "Sears doesn't exist anymore, George," she said. "Anyway, what are you getting at?"

"I'm trying to think of places my grandma shops," George replied. "Because this crowd is . . . seasoned."

I looked around. George had a point. There was an abundance of gray hair, canes, walkers, even an oxygen tank or two. As I was stepping to the side to look down the hall, I bumped into someone. "Oh! Sorry!"

An older woman in a bright red jumpsuit turned to face me and scowled. "*Do* watch where you're going, please! Anyway, what were you saying, Barb?" She held up an enormous smartphone in a rubber case.

Another older woman, this one with long gray hair braided down her back, pointed at the screen. "Is there a download button? Can you save it?"

The first woman groaned. "I did that already. And then it just goes away! I don't know where it saves or . . ." She let out a frustrated sound, then shoved the phone back in her purse. "Forget it. If she really wants me to have it, she'll send it in the mail or as a fax."

I stepped back toward Bess and George, who were now eyeballing the buffet. "They still have the shrimp at lunch?" George asked. "For *$4.99?*"

"There are crab legs over there too," Bess said, pointing.

George shook her head. "Dang," she was saying. "I know we ate all the eggs in Vegas for breakfast, but I could *almost* be hungry again, for . . ."

But I wasn't listening—because something was clicking in my brain. "That's it!" I said, grabbing Bess's hand and then George's. "Guys—I've just thought of our plan B."

A few minutes later, I hesitantly approached the check-in desk. Like the buffet, it was busy and chaotic. It looked like a whole flight crew had recently arrived and the staff was just finishing up checking them in. I waited in line, looking around the lobby. I'd sent Bess and George back to the room to wait for me. This was an errand I should do alone—the less attention I brought to myself, the better.

After a little while, the desk clerk on the left finished with her flight attendant and nodded me over. "Can I help you?" she asked.

I took a quick scan of the clerk. She looked to be in her midtwenties, with dark curls and dimples, and her name tag read DIANA. Most importantly, I hadn't seen her before. I could only hope that she hadn't been working the day before or that she didn't know enough about Veronica's disappearance to recognize her room number.

"I hope so," I said, shooting her an ingratiating smile. "See, I'm a personal assistant, and I'm in deep sneakers with my new boss, Ronny. She's *furious* with me because I spilled soda on a fax she received a couple of days ago and it blurred the ink."

Diana's brows scrunched up. "A fax?" she asked.

"That's right," I said, leaning in with an *I know, right?* chuckle in my voice. "Who knew faxes even still *exist*, right? Like, just email it. But Ronny works with some older clients, and they still love their fax machines."

I watched Diana's face, scanning for any signs that she was suspicious. Did the casino even *have* a fax machine? I was hoping so. When we'd encountered the older woman in the buffet line, it hit me: the man I'd spoken to on the phone last night sounded older. And older people don't always send "documents" in ways that can be accessed by a smartphone. He might have mailed it, but that would have been tricky, timing it so that it arrived at the casino in time for Veronica to receive it, but without Xavier finding out.

A fax would be easier. It could be sent with the push of a button, and Veronica could just be alerted to go pick it up at the front desk.

But faxes had another important property. Unlike emailed documents, they weren't stored in cyber-space until deleted. But fax machines *did* have a small amount of memory. And, if my Google search hadn't led me astray, faxes could be reprinted—*if* you tried to do it soon after the original fax was sent.

Now Diana was looking behind me, and her mouth was tight, the dimples gone. I glanced back. Oh no. Twenty or so more flight attendants and crew had appeared out of nowhere, and they all looked impatient.

She turned back to me and sighed. "What's the room number?"

I gave her Veronica's suite, then waited as she hustled through a door behind the desk. I could only hope that if the fax reprinted, Veronica's name wasn't prominent on it. Or that Diana was too preoccupied to recognize that it was the name of the bride who had disappeared the night before.

A minute or so later, she reappeared, a manila envelope in her hand. She strode back to me and pushed the envelope across the desk.

"Don't spill soda on this one, okay? *Next!*"

I backed away, trying not to stare weirdly at the envelope. I couldn't quite believe my luck. *The mystery texter* did *send a fax! And I have it now! Plan B actually led somewhere!*

But before I could waste too much time, I hustled back to the elevator and pushed the button for our room. I couldn't wait to show Bess and George what I'd found . . . and hopefully how much closer we were to finding Veronica.

CHAPTER NINE

Fax are Fax

"OMIGOSH, OMIGOSH, OMIGOSH," BESS cried as I slipped past her into our room, holding up my manila envelope of recovered fax pages. "Are you serious? I can't believe that *worked*!"

"In all fairness, I think I was helped by the massive airline crew that was checking in behind me," I said, sitting down on my bed. George was already lying on the one she shared with Bess, watching me with bright eyes. "The clerk was in a hurry to get rid of me."

"Who *faxes* anymore?" George asked, shaking her head. "Who even knew the hotel *had* a fax?"

"It's a perfectly legitimate way to send information," Bess said, coming over to sit next to me on the bed. "Don't be a techie snob, George. What if you needed to send someone a document ASAP, but they didn't have a computer?"

"Or a phone?" George asked incredulously. "Or access to a computer, like, in the hotel business center?"

I held up a hand. "Guys! We're not solving the mystery of whether faxes are the best way to send information. I think history has weighed in on that one. We *are* trying to solve the mystery of where your cousin is." I ripped open the envelope. "Let's hope this will shed some light on that."

I pulled out a sheaf of ten or so pages, including a cover note. *Veronica, I know you love him, but I hope you will take this seriously. Love, Uncle Felix.*

"Who's Felix?" I asked, glancing between Bess and George. "Do we know?"

"Uhhh, sort of," Bess replied, screwing up her face like she was trying to remember something but couldn't quite get there. "I think he's, like, my uncle's uncle?

He's one of the older relatives I hear about sometimes. I'm not sure I've ever met him."

"So that would make him . . . ?" I tried to think.

"Veronica's great-uncle," George replied. When I looked at her, impressed, she added, "Please don't ask what he is to us—I don't know."

"He's a guy named Felix," I said, pushing the cover note aside. "Okay, Felix, what were you trying to tell Veronica?"

I pored through the documents. So many numbers! The first few pages were what looked like the summary of a tax return for the Redd Zone. It had been prepared by one Felix Romero—so he must have been Redd Zone's accountant as well as Veronica's great-uncle.

"Should I know what this means?" I asked, looking at the long columns of numbers.

"Give it to me," George suggested, holding out her hands. I held out the pages and she took them.

Her eyes scanned rapidly back and forth, and she flipped one page forward, then another. "Huh."

She didn't look happy. In fact, with each page she scanned, her frown was deepening. "Wow." Finally she looked up.

"Well," she said. "To make a long story short: Redd Zone is losing money. A *lot* of money. You might say that Redd Zone is *really* in the red!"

The corners of her mouth quirked up, and her eyes brightened. I could tell George thought she had made some killer pun, but I wasn't following.

"Lame, cuz," Bess said, shaking her head. "Leave the puns to me. We all know I'm the funny cousin."

I waved my hand in a *let's put that aside for now* gesture. "George, explain to me how they're losing money," I said. "It seems like Xavier and Veronica are spending a ton of it this weekend, right? All these extreme-sports stunts. Didn't Max say they were super expensive?"

George nodded, flipping through the faxed pages. "Yeah, and he's right. You need insurance, permits, all kinds of things. I can't tell you why they did that. What I *can* tell you is that they're deeply in debt."

Bess frowned. "But didn't they just expand the complex earlier this year? It was a big addition too—making it the largest extreme-sports complex in Chicago. Why would they do that if they were losing money? Why make a *bigger* store if you're not making enough money in your little store?"

George sighed, looking between a few pages. "Because . . . they're bad at business? I can't tell you, honestly. Maybe they thought that a bigger store would be more visible and bring in more customers. Maybe they were trying to be bigger than their competition. But either way, it looks like that expansion, which cost quite a bit, was paid for with loans. They were already losing money, but they decided to expand the store anyway."

Hmm. That seemed . . . pretty foolish, honestly. And Xavier and Max didn't seem like fools. I stared at my lap, trying to puzzle that out.

Bess tilted her head. "Is that what they call throwing good money after bad?"

George raised an eyebrow over the page she was

reading. "I think that's exactly what they call it. And I hate to say this, but according to these documents, they appear to be close to bankruptcy."

Bess groaned, and I squirmed uncomfortably on the bed. "Do you guys think Veronica knew?" I asked. "Max and Xavier definitely give the appearance of a very successful store, but maybe that's only to people they don't know well. Bess, you're closer to Veronica than we are. Did she ever say anything to you hinting that, you know, Xavier's finances weren't in the best shape?"

Bess looked thoughtful, then shook her head. "No, actually, just the opposite," she said. "She's said a few times that he's this smart, successful businessman, and that's part of what attracted her to him. She's going into a low-paid career, so it makes her feel safe to be marrying someone who's good with money." She sighed. "You know, her family struggled a little when she was younger. I think it was a big deal to her that Xavier seemed financially secure. Plus, she liked that he was so good at something he clearly loves."

George put down the faxed pages. "Ugh, poor Veronica," she murmured. "Finding this major news out, like, the day before her wedding . . ."

Everyone was quiet for a few seconds, then we all looked up at the same time.

"That's why she ran, right?" I asked. "It has to be. The revelations about his finances made her not want to marry him anymore?"

Bess bit her lip, and George sighed pensively.

"I don't know," Bess said after a moment. "I'm telling you guys, she seemed totally in love to me. *Totally* in love. And Veronica was looking forward to a secure life, but I don't think she's the kind of person to leave someone because they're poor. I think she would have wanted to figure it out together."

"Well then, maybe she was worried about her own money," I suggested. "When you get married, you're joining yourselves not just legally, but financially, too. Could Veronica have been worried that Xavier was marrying her so that he could use her money to bail him out?"

"What money?" Bess scoffed. "Veronica's one of those people who can't stop studying. She's been a student for years and years. She's getting her master's in social work now. Trust me, her net worth is in the negative numbers too."

George nodded. "Yeah, if Xavier was trying to marry for money, he picked the wrong girl. She has a ton of student debt."

"They were marrying for love," Bess added, folding her arms in front of her. "I'm *sure* of it."

We all fell silent again.

"It *does*," George said finally, raising a pointer finger, "make you wonder about the risks he was taking. You know, like Priya's been saying all along."

I thought back to the BASE jumping disaster—how Max had been filming it the whole time. Just like he'd filmed the flyboarding at the cocktail hour. And Xavier's troubling post from his hospital bed, making it seem like he had no regrets, and was even using his accident to gather likes and follows.

"Maybe Priya was onto something," I suggested.

"Maybe he *has* been escalating the risks he and Veronica have been taking—because he felt he *had* to, to save his brand."

Bess nodded. "Because he was trying to build himself as an influencer," she added. "Maybe he thought if he got enough followers, he could turn enough of them into customers to save the Redd Zone."

George wrinkled her nose and reached into her pocket. "*Speaking* of which . . ." She pulled out her phone, clicked on Instagram, and scrolled through a few posts. Sure enough, a familiar face appeared pretty quickly.

It was Xavier, posting a video on the Redd Zone account from his hotel room. He stared out the window forlornly, glancing down at the camera only every few seconds. *Still missing* was written at the top of the page. "Day two," he announced, "and still no Veronica. I can't really express to you guys how much I miss her. This is killing me. I just keep asking myself, what could I have . . ."

George flicked her finger across the video, scrolling down.

"Hey!" Bess said. "He was still . . ."

But George kept scrolling. "I know, guys. But it looks like he's posted five of these, today alone."

I stared at the screen. George was right. Most of her feed was taken up by Redd Zone videos. And as she quickly clicked on each one, they all seemed to have a common theme: poor Xavier, this was so hard on him, what was he supposed to do about their wedding gifts or honeymoon? "I hope we can still make it to Costa Rica someday . . . *together*," he finished in one post, covering his eyes and letting out a sob.

"Is that fake crying?" George asked. "I can't tell."

"Oh, *George*," Bess snapped, frowning at her cousin. "Let's assume he's really crying, okay? He just lost his fiancée."

"I *know*," George replied, gesturing to her feed. "At this rate, I don't think anyone on Instagram *doesn't* know."

I sighed. "I want to believe Xavier is for real too Bess," I said. "But . . . I don't love that he posts so much. It makes me wonder if he's faking it for likes and views.

And I remember how upset Veronica looked when we saw her on the observation deck the night before the wedding, after his accident. I can't help thinking maybe Priya really was onto something. Maybe Veronica saw all this financial data, saw him nearly die BASE jumping, and started to worry that Xavier would just keep filming them doing crazy stunts, escalating the risk each time, until it killed one of them."

George looked thoughtful. "I think we can agree," she said, clicking the button to darken her phone, "that his relationship with social media is not healthy."

Bess shook her head. "But lots of people overshare," she insisted. "That doesn't make them *unmarryable*. And I just have to believe, if Veronica was starting to doubt the person he was, she would have said something to somebody. Maybe not me, maybe that would have been uncomfortable because I was her younger cousin. But *somebody*."

Bess frowned down into her lap, but I glanced over and caught George's eye. She looked like she'd just thought of something.

"You know," she said, "actually, I can think of two somebodies we can ask. . . ."

She unlocked her phone again and opened the messages app. As Bess and I watched, she typed in *Priya*, then *Deanna*.

Hey girls, she typed into the text box. We're all feeling a little stressed about Veronica. Want to have coffee and talk about it?

CHAPTER TEN

Not Awkward
at All

WHEN PRIYA AND DEANNA RESPONDED, WE all decided via group text that we could use a break from the casino. George found a cute café on a side street a short walk to the north, in the opposite direction of the bigger casinos. We decided to meet up there a few hours later.

It did feel good to get away from the Soar for the first time in nearly two days. It was nice to see the sky, to feel the sun on our faces, even if that sun was unbearably hot. It made me realize how the casinos were these little self-contained worlds, with restaurants and entertainment and everything you could possibly need. They were designed not to be left, but it felt good to leave.

I hoped Veronica, wherever she was, could feel the sun on her face too.

Deanna was waiting at a table when we arrived. She looked stressed out, with heavy bags under her eyes. She wasn't wearing any makeup, which was unusual for her. Her hair was pulled into a messy topknot, and she wore jogging shorts with an oversize Homer Simpson tank top. She was sipping a huge iced coffee.

"Hey," she said when we sat down to join her. "I hope it's okay I ordered ahead. I needed the caffeine."

George leaned in to give her a hug. "No worries," she said. "How have you been holding up?"

Deanna gave a short laugh that sounded more like a sob at the end. "Not great?" she said. "I mean, I haven't been sleeping. I just keep thinking about what happened to Veronica. Who could have taken her."

"*Taken*," I repeated, pulling over a menu. "So you don't think she left on her own?"

Deanna's eyes flashed to me, looking slightly annoyed. I could see the redness around them now. "I don't," she said. "I mean, I know she changed out of her gown or whatever Xavier says. But I know my sister, and I know she loves that man. Besides, there's no way she would have disappeared without telling *me*. I don't know what was going on with her, but I just don't believe . . ."

She was looking behind me, and her voice trailed off. I turned around to see what she was looking at and spotted Priya, who had just entered, wearing a pretty orange sundress and carrying a shopping bag. She pushed her sunglasses back on her head and ran over to us.

"Hey, guys," she said, shooting a tentative look at Deanna, who just stared at her. "Sorry I'm late. I've been stress-shopping."

"Stress-shopping?" Deanna asked incredulously. "Is that a thing?"

Priya shrugged and sat down in the one remaining chair. "Just, you know, like all of you, I guess, I feel kind of restless and rattled. We're supposed to fly home tomorrow, and I don't want to, but the kids have school and we have work and I don't know what to do here, really. I don't know what to do with myself. I wish I knew where Veronica was, and I want to help, but I don't know how. So I went to the mall in the Gully Ranch casino and spent way too much money on cute kids' clothes."

Deanna's eyes widened, but she didn't say anything.

"Obviously, neither one of you have heard from her since the wedding, right?" I asked.

Deanna shook her head. Priya said no and quickly began scanning the menu.

The table seemed to be filled with a weird, awkward tension. Deanna kept looking at Priya like she was vaguely disgusted, but Priya didn't seem to notice. She looked at the menu for a few minutes, then asked if we were all ready to order. The waitress came over, and we all ordered food except for Deanna, who said she'd stick with the iced coffee.

"I don't have much of an appetite lately," she said as

the waitress walked away, shooting a pointed glance at Priya. "You know, since my *sister was kidnapped.*"

Priya looked up at her in surprise, her mouth in a neat, pink-rimmed *O*. "Kidnapped?" she asked. "I mean, I understand we don't know where she is, and that's a concern. But she had that disguise stashed in the restroom, and she got into the elevator herself. Isn't it more likely she finally came to her senses?"

Now Deanna's mouth dropped open.

"What do you mean, Priya?" Bess asked quickly. "Did Veronica tell you something before the wedding that makes you think that?"

"Yeah, I guess . . . ," George added awkwardly, "I guess we're hoping the two of you can fill us in on how Veronica was feeling right before the wedding. We know what she said—or *didn't* say—to us, but Bess and I are just her little cousins. You're her sister and her best friend. You two know her better than anybody."

Deanna and Priya looked at each other, as though each was silently daring the other to go first. Finally Priya shifted in her seat and spoke up. "I met her at the hospital," she said. "I asked my husband to drop me off on his way back to the Soar. I think it's fair to say she was shaken?" She seemed to be asking Deanna.

Deanna looked a bit defensive, but nodded slowly. "Yeah, I mean, like anyone would be. Extreme sports have risks, even when you know what you're doing. But you never really get used to close calls like that."

Priya cleared her throat. "She was relieved and happy Xavier was alive, obviously," she went on. "But I sensed something else. She seemed . . . really thrown by it. You know, she couldn't even stay at the hospital with him, she was so upset. Once she learned he would be okay and he just needed a bone set, she wanted to come back to the casino with me. And when we got here, I tried to get her to talk to me, but she said no. She wanted to be alone."

George looked pensive. "So what do you think that meant?" she asked Priya. "What was she upset about?"

Priya's eyes widened. "Isn't it obvious?" she asked. "I feel like I keep saying the same thing. I think she finally saw him for what he was. That this wasn't going to change. That if she married him, it would just be a parade of near misses, a string of visits to different hospitals. Until one day maybe he isn't so lucky."

Bess frowned. "So you think she left willingly, because her feelings for him changed," she suggested.

Priya nodded. "I think she finally saw the truth," she said, looking at Deanna. "So I'm sorry—I'm sorry if I don't seem stressed out enough, or worried enough. But honestly? I feel *happy* for Veronica. I think she made the right choice for herself, for the Veronica that I know."

Deanna coughed. "Well, the Veronica *I* know called me that night, after you brought her back to the Soar," she said, pausing to sip her iced coffee. "And her take on things was a little different."

All eyes jumped to Deanna. Even Priya looked surprised and curious.

"What did Veronica say?" I asked.

Deanna shrugged. "She *was* freaked out, that's true—but not because her feelings had changed for Xavier. She was really freaked out for him, really relieved he was okay. But the reaction Priya saw, how upset she was—that wasn't because of anything Xavier did. It was because his accident could have happened to her."

Priya stared at her. "Well, of course. That's what I'm saying. Since she met Xavier, I was always worried about her dying in a bungee jump or skydiving or— whatever! All the risks he took, he convinced *her* to—"

Deanna held up a finger to stop her. "No, listen to me. I'm not talking about the general risks of extreme sports. *This literal accident* could have happened to her. Because the suit he used, the one where the parachute failed? It was supposed to be hers."

"What?" Priya cried, and I think we all jumped a little. We were all stunned, but the rest of us absorbed this in silence. I looked at Bess and George, my heart beating a mile a minute, trying to telegraph with my eyes: *Why would they switch suits? This has to play into her running!*

Deanna took another sip of her iced coffee and nodded. "Xavier noticed that it didn't fit her well. He thought it was a little too stretched out in the arms and legs. So he switched with her. And thank God he did, because I'm not sure she would have known to fly into the tree to save herself. She's still new to all this stuff. He's the old pro. So while the whole incident was scary, I think it worked out as well as it could have."

Priya's mouth had dropped open again, and she waved her arm disbelievingly. "Doesn't that prove my point, though? She was realizing how much danger Xavier puts her in! She could have *died*!"

"No," Deanna said, shaking her head. "Uh-uh. The girl I talked to the night before the wedding was still *crazy* in love with that man. She was working through some stuff, sure. But there wasn't one bone in Veronica's body that didn't want to marry him," she insisted. "She would never put him through this. There's only one reason Veronica would have run out on her wedding, and that's because someone forced her."

As the waitress arrived with our food, breaking the tension, a thought occurred to me. We all began eating, and I turned to Deanna.

"What do you know about Arlo?" I asked.

She looked surprised. "Arlo Graham? Xavier's old friend?"

I nodded. "I spoke to him at the rehearsal dinner. He talked about wanting to go into business with Xavier, but when he got out of prison, Xavier already had the Redd Zone."

Priya grunted in agreement. "Right, and then there was that strange toast he made. About how you can't count on Xavier?"

Deanna looked amused, but I pressed on. "Is there any reason he might have wanted to hurt Xavier? Maybe he's holding on to old grudges?"

She gave me a wry look. "Arlo? He's a weird guy, but no. I've met him before, and he and Xavier always have that kind of energy together—they tease hard. What Arlo said at the rehearsal dinner didn't ring my alarm bells at all."

I took that in, but I wasn't sure I was convinced. I couldn't forget the odd vibe I'd gotten from Arlo. Even though there hadn't been any texts on Veronica's phone, she *had* spoken to somebody from the elevator. Maybe they'd planned it in person. Could he have done something to Veronica?

The rest of the meeting passed awkwardly, but blessedly quickly. I was eager to get back to our room and talk with Bess and George about what we'd learned. Maybe even make some lists, go through some suspects. Both Priya and Deanna made good cases, but Deanna's conviction that the night before the wedding, Veronica wanted to marry Xavier was making an impression on me.

Had I accepted too easily that she had left willingly? Could someone have coerced her into changing and getting into the elevator, then met her on the restaurant floor to force her to go—somewhere? If not Arlo, someone else?

We thanked Priya and Deanna and hustled back to the Soar. I think Bess, George, and I had all made a silent agreement not to talk about it until we were alone, but once we got back to our room and shut the door behind us, we all erupted at once.

"What if Deanna is right and someone—" I began just as George cried, "I think maybe Veronica got scared, scared enough to—" and Bess said simply, "Guys, I'm really worried. I'm worried that Xavier tried to kill her."

That shut George and me up pretty quickly.

"*What?*" George asked. "You've been, like, Team Xavier this whole time."

Bess nodded, her eyes wide. "That's because I know how much Veronica loved him. But people love the wrong person all the time. Just because someone loves you doesn't make you innocent. And I just keep flashing back to a combination of Priya saying something changed in Veronica at the hospital—and Deanna saying that Veronica knew it could have been her. She knew he changed the suits."

"What do you mean?" I asked. "If Xavier tampered with the suit, why would he have changed them and taken the damaged one?"

Bess shook her head and shrugged. "Maybe in the end, he couldn't do it? And he thought he knew enough about BASE jumping to survive the fall? Maybe he maneuvered into a tree on purpose."

I didn't know what to say to that.

"But maybe Veronica was afraid he might not get cold feet the next time," Bess added.

I dropped my purse on Bess and George's bed and stared at her. I had been looking in the complete opposite direction, at guests who might have conspired with Veronica to convince her to leave. But Bess's theory, although wonky, wasn't completely unbelievable. I'd spent enough time with Xavier by now to feel that he *did* really care about Veronica. Still, what if he had some other motive to want her dead? What if the most obvious suspect was the right one? "If she thought he'd tried to kill her, that would definitely explain running away at the wedding," I said.

"And not telling anyone," George added. "If she was scared of what he might do."

"Oh, poor Veronica," Bess moaned, sitting down on her bed. "But . . . why would he do it? He seems to really care about her!"

"Unless he's an *incredible* actor," George pointed out. "Which is possible. Sociopaths can be very charming."

"We know about his debt," I reminded them. "So I guess the question is . . . is there a way he could get money from Veronica's death?"

We were all quiet as we thought that through.

"Not really," George said finally. "Not as her fiancé, anyway. If they were married, he could have taken out a life insurance policy on her. Then if she died, he, her next of kin, would get a big payout."

"And all his problems would be solved," I said, nodding. It wasn't an uncommon crime, if those true crime news documentaries that aired on the weekends were to be believed. And as horrible as it was to think that Xavier might look at killing his bride as a money-making opportunity, I could at least see the logic of it. But it still didn't make sense. "They weren't married yet. And I just can't get past the idea that if this theory is true, he took the suit with the disabled parachute on purpose. He would know he was putting his life in danger," I said. "Would anyone take that big of a risk, even for someone they love?"

BANG BANG BANG!

We all jumped about a foot in the air as a startlingly loud sound filled the room. It took me a minute to realize someone was knocking on our door—*really* hard.

With a nervous glance at me and Bess, George stood up to open it. Bess and I got up to follow her.

"Oh, hey." It was Xavier. Or rather, it was Xavier with two police officers and a trio of security guards fanned out behind him. One of them was Flora, the head of the whole security department. *What's going on?* "Did I scare you? I'm sorry. It's just—"

Flora stepped forward. "Come with me," she said brusquely. "It's regarding Veronica's disappearance. I'm afraid we've found something disturbing."

CHAPTER ELEVEN

~

The Picture
Changes

WITHIN MINUTES, BESS, GEORGE, AND I were back in the small room off the larger security center of the casino, where we had first viewed the video footage on a laptop. This time, we had Xavier standing behind us as Flora typed onto the laptop herself.

"I'm sorry we didn't notice this earlier," Flora said, cueing up a video. "I hope, when you see it, you'll understand why."

She pressed play and the image began moving. It was from inside a huge parking garage—the one beneath the Soar, I assumed. Two large men exited a door marked STAIRWAY D and looked around warily. When they shifted their positions, I gasped. It was easy to miss, but they were leading—more like *dragging*—a smaller figure between them. The smaller figure had an LA Dodgers cap pulled down, obscuring her face and hair, but her outfit was the same one Veronica had put on when she'd changed in the restroom near the observation deck.

"Veronica," Bess breathed. "Oh my gosh. Deanna was right!"

As the larger men pulled the smaller person along, it became clear that her hands were bound. For one split second, she raised her head to maneuver around a parked pickup truck, and we could see the expression on her face.

It was undoubtedly Veronica, still in her older-lady disguise. And she looked terrified.

"Stairway D doesn't have any security cameras," Flora explained. "It's mainly used by staff. And the new baseball cap on Veronica made it easy to miss her. But it does appear that she didn't leave the Soar willingly."

We all fell silent, staring at the video, which now showed the men loading Veronica into a white van and driving away. Xavier broke our silence with a cry.

"What are you going to *do* about this?" he demanded, turning to the police. "Here's hard evidence that the love of my life was abducted and dragged out of this casino. And because we just found this, they've had a whole day to do whatever it is they planned on doing!"

"She could be in Mexico by now," George agreed, shaking her head. When Xavier turned to her, looking devastated, she whispered, "Sorry . . . but she could."

The police officers were a middle-aged Latina woman with short, curly hair whose badge read LOPEZ, and a young white guy with a blond crew cut whose badge read WHIPPLE. The woman stepped forward. "Look," she said, "we can imagine how you feel. This has been a tricky case since the beginning, because we couldn't be sure that your fiancée didn't leave on her own terms. This video casts things in a different light. We'll step up our efforts, of course. It's a shame we can't see the license plate in this video, because that would give us a way in."

"We'll keep looking," Flora promised. "It's possible another camera caught it on its way out. But I can't make promises."

Officer Whipple nodded. "We'll keep trying to identify the men, too," he promised. "Flora found some additional footage of them on the third floor, where it looks like they were waiting for Veronica. Mr. Redd, again, just to be sure, you have no idea who these men could be?"

Xavier turned to him and shook his head dramatically. "I told you, I have no idea. I don't know anybody in Vegas, and I *definitely* don't know anyone who looks like that."

Officer Lopez stepped toward him. "Is there anyone you can think of who'd want to hurt you?" she asked gently. "Or Veronica? Anyone who might be looking for revenge?"

Xavier stared at her, looking pained, and then groaned and shook his head. "No! I don't have enemies, man!" he cried. "Neither does Veronica! I can't imagine why anyone would do this. That's what makes this all so hard to take."

I cleared my throat and turned awkwardly to Xavier. "What about Arlo?" I asked.

Xavier scowled. He looked upset that I was even suggesting Arlo might have had something to do with it.

"I know, I know," I said quickly. "He's an old friend. But his speech at the rehearsal dinner seemed—I don't know—bitter, maybe? Is he maybe a little resentful that you started the Redd Zone without him?"

Xavier seemed to consider that, then shook his head almost sadly. "No, he isn't. Arlo has a weird sense of humor. He and I are tough on each other. But that's my *brother*, man. Besides, he was with me every second of the wedding day. He couldn't have been setting this up."

"It's possible that these men could be working for someone," Officer Lopez said, gesturing to the now-paused video. "It would only take a few seconds to text or call and set this in motion. Could your friend have set this up in advance, or . . ."

"*No!*" Xavier shouted, cutting her off. "Look, everyone thinks Arlo is up to something because he's just out of prison. But he's on probation, man. He has to check in with his parole officer all the time. And he could get in a lot of trouble for talking to hit men or goons or whoever the heck you hire to kidnap a grown woman. I just *know* he didn't do it. And every second you spend on him is going to take time away from finding whoever really has Veronica."

I stared at Xavier for a moment, then looked at Bess and George. They looked as thoughtful as I felt. Was Xavier really sure he could trust his friend so completely? Or did he know Arlo *didn't* do it because Xavier was the one who did?

Officer Whipple put a hand on Xavier's shoulder. "I'm sorry," he said. "Look, we're going to find her."

Xavier shook his head, looking at the ground. "I knew it," he said. "I told you all. Veronica would never have left me on purpose! Our love is real!"

Officer Lopez shared a glance with Officer Whipple, then nodded encouragingly. "Don't worry, Mr. Redd," she said. "We'll find your fiancée."

"Wife," Xavier cut in quickly, still facing the floor. "Veronica is my wife."

The rest of us exchanged confused looks. We all knew the wedding hadn't happened. *Is he okay?*

"Well, she *would* have been," Flora countered. "I guess I'm confused. You never actually exchanged vows, did you?"

Xavier looked up at us then. His face was dead serious. "No, she was my wife," he said simply. "Legally, emotionally, however you want to put it. It was her idea. She's not always comfortable with my whole . . ." He made a vague jazz-hands sort of gesture. "Social media presence," he finished awkwardly.

George gave him a pointed look. "What does that have to do with you getting married?" she asked.

Xavier met her gaze and sighed. "She was afraid the wedding would be too much of a spectacle," he explained. "You know, with the extreme sports and posting it all for our followers. She said she wanted a moment that was just for *us*. So yeah, we had a private wedding a couple of weeks ago on the lakeshore in Chicago."

Bess threw up her hands. "You're already married? You got married *before* your wedding?"

George looked thoughtful. "It's actually sort of . . . romantic," she murmured.

"It was," Xavier agreed. "Just us, two witnesses, and a justice of the peace."

It *did* sound romantic. But my mind was going in another direction entirely. It was going back to our conversation just before the police banged on our door . . . about why Veronica had been so upset the night before. About the switched suits. About the looming bankruptcy.

About how Veronica's death could possibly benefit Xavier.

I coughed. "Sorry . . . this was a legal marriage?" I pressed. "You and Veronica really are husband and wife?"

"Absolutely," Xavier replied. "Why get married if it's not legal?"

I glanced over at Bess and George and managed to catch George's eye. She looked pensive, and then suddenly her eyes widened. I could tell she was putting together exactly what I was.

If Xavier and Veronica were already married . . . he could have a life insurance policy out on her. And if she dies, he gets a hefty check . . . and all of Redd Zone's problems are solved.

She elbowed Bess and gave her a knowing look. I watched as Bess seemed to get it too, her mouth dropping open.

Then they both looked at me. Bess gave me a stare that seemed to burn into my skin. *Say something,* she mouthed. *You have to.*

I did. She was right. But how, right here, in front of Xavier? I cleared my throat, trying to work up the courage.

"There's, uh, someth—" I began.

But almost immediately, I was cut off by a blaring

ringtone. Xavier shoved his hand into his pocket and pulled out his smartphone, then frowned at the screen.

He held up his index finger to the cops. "Sorry," he said. "I need to take this. Give me just a minute."

And before anybody could say anything, he'd ducked out of the room.

Officer Lopez looked at me. "Were you saying something, miss?" she asked.

Miss. Wow, the police usually talk to me like I'm a kid. "I was," I said, nodding and screwing up my courage. "See, I'm sort of a part-time sleuth. Not professionally, but, like, it's just who I am? Anyway, I've been doing some investigating of my own, and I think there's something you should know. . . ."

CHAPTER TWELVE

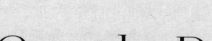

Caught Redd Handed

I WASN'T SURE WHERE TO START, SO I JUST plunged in. "Redd Zone is broke," I announced. When I was met by five blank stares, I added, "That's Xavier's business."

Officer Lopez looked confused. "Xavier, Xavier?" she asked, pointing to the door where the man in question had recently disappeared. "The husband? The guy we were just talking to?"

I nodded.

"Okay, what does that have to do with his wife's abduction?" she asked.

I tried to explain. The financial documents faxed to Veronica by a concerned relative, just nights before the wedding. The escalating danger of the extreme sports they were doing, and the fact that she and Xavier switched BASE jumping suits just moments before his parachute failed and he landed in a tree. Finally, the fact that they were secretly married . . .

"Which means he could have a life insurance policy out on her," I concluded. "That could give him a motive to hurt her. If Veronica dies, Xavier could cash in, and all of Redd Zone's financial problems would just"—I made a tiny explosion with my hand—"poof!"

Officer Lopez and Officer Whipple looked at each other. I could see the wariness in their eyes: *This so-called teenage detective thinks she knows what she's talking about?* But as my words sank in, I could see the look in their eyes changing from wariness to grudging acceptance. *This so-called teenage detective knows what she's talking about. Shoot. What now?*

"It tracks," Officer Whipple said with a nod. "I hate to say it, but we have no other suspects who even come close to that kind of motive to hurt the victim. I'm going to call in to the station and see if they can track down a policy."

As he pulled out his phone and left the room, presumably to find better reception, relief washed over me. If I can make a good case, *usually* local law enforcement takes me seriously, but it's definitely not a sure thing. *They're taking it seriously! Phew!*

But I also dreaded Xavier's reaction. He seemed like a good guy. I mean, a lot of crooks seem like good guys; I should know that better than anybody. Still, it didn't feel great to believe that Xavier would have wanted to hurt Veronica. I'd come here to attend a wedding, not prevent a murder. And had it even been prevented? We didn't know where Veronica was, or whether she was safe.

Officer Lopez nodded. "Thank you, Nancy. And speak of the devil, where *is* Xavier? His phone call seems to be a long one." She frowned suspiciously in the direction of the door he'd left through. "I think I'd better go find Mr. Redd."

She hustled through the door, leaving Bess, George, and me alone with Flora and the other security guards.

Flora was regarding me with a slow smile. "You're not half-bad at this," she said admiringly. "Do you like Vegas? Ever think about a career in casino security?"

"Not really," I said honestly. "But you know, I'm still pretty—"

The door swung open and Officer Lopez charged through, her mouth tight. "That sneaky little . . ." She sighed and shook her head. "No sign of him anywhere. I don't know why I'm surprised."

"Xavier's gone?" Bess asked. She looked disappointed. I guessed I wasn't the only one having trouble accepting that Xavier was our bad guy.

"Yeah, unless he went *outside* outside to take a phone call," Officer Lopez replied. "But it seems more likely—"

The door burst open again, this time revealing a red-faced Officer Whipple. He looked at us all looking at him expectantly and shook his head.

"It's bad news," he said. "The station found a life

insurance policy taken out on Veronica just four days ago."

Oh nooooo. I felt my whole body sink. *I was right.* But I didn't really want to be right. I wanted Veronica to be okay. I wanted Xavier to be a good guy. I wanted a happy ending!

Officer Lopez looked upset too. "How much?" she asked.

"One point five million dollars," Officer Whipple replied.

Officer Lopez shook her head, swore, and then looked to Flora. "We have to lock down the casino," she said. "This might be an attempted murder. Until our suspect is found, no one leaves or enters."

Flora pulled a walkie-talkie out of her vest. "On it," she replied. "Let's find this crook!"

Squad cars full of city cops squealed into the Soar's driveway, and within minutes no one was allowed to enter or leave the building. The police blocked each entrance and exit, then searched the entire casino, the hotel, the restaurants, the observation deck, and the rides. They searched every car in the parking garage, opened storage closets, pored through every kitchen in every café. They knocked on the door of every hotel room and searched backstage at the Stratosphere Cabaret Theater (resident performer: the Amazing Jamie Figman, hypnotist to the stars).

They didn't find Xavier anywhere. With every update, my gut seemed to sink lower. This couldn't be a misunderstanding. He'd sensed me getting too close to the truth and run. Which meant he had to have taken Veronica, and if she was still alive, he had to know where she was.

Now that I knew she'd been abducted, my mind whirled with places she might have been taken. What Xavier might have wanted to do with her. If he'd switched BASE jumping suits with her, did that mean he'd really had a change of heart and couldn't bring himself to hurt her? Were his conspirators holding her someplace, waiting to decide what to do next? Was that who had called him?

Or had he abducted her for a much darker purpose . . . to finish the job he'd been unable to complete at the rehearsal dinner?

I felt like my insides were tied up in knots. What if I'd figured this out earlier? Would the police find her in time? Would they find her at all?

Bess, George, and I were sitting in a small lounge area off the hotel lobby, trying to keep our panic in check.

"What if she *did* get wise to Xavier and try to run—and he caught her anyway?" George asked emotionally. "She had that disguise ready. She probably thought she was home free."

Bess shook her head. "I can't think about that. I have to believe she's still okay somewhere."

"Maybe he planned to kill her but couldn't go through with the plan," I suggested. "Remember, we still don't know why he switched suits with her for the BASE jump. But that could mean he had regrets, right? Maybe when it came right down to it, he couldn't hurt her."

"*That* time," George put in, shaking her head and blinking rapidly, as if trying to keep back tears. "He couldn't kill her *that* time. But who knows what could have happened after that?"

Suddenly footsteps came running down the hallway, and soon two familiar faces came around the corner to face us: Officers Lopez and Whipple.

"We've found something," Officer Whipple said breathlessly.

Moving closer to us, he quickly explained that a report had come in from a beat cop working on the Strip. Xavier had been spotted in a Rent a Ride garage across the street from the Polynesian casino. He and Officer Lopez had the license plate of the car Xavier had driven away in, as well as the make and model—a silver '21 Chevy Malibu.

"He can't have gotten far," Officer Lopez was saying. "He'd just pulled the car out of the driveway when this was called in to us."

I jumped to my feet. "So what now?" I asked, glancing toward the Soar's circular driveway. I knew it wasn't exactly standard procedure for police officers to take teenage sleuths and their cohorts along on high-speed chases. But I also couldn't imagine how hard it would be to stay in that hotel lobby, biting our finger-nails down to the quick and just praying that Veronica would be found okay. "Can we . . . come with you?"

Officer Lopez looked me up and down. She let out a deep sigh. Then she leaned in like she was going to tell me a secret.

"If anyone asks you, this never happened," she hissed. "But yeah, all right, come with us. The three of you. Come on. Hurry."

I glanced back at George and Bess, who looked as relieved as I felt. We all darted along after the cops and followed them to a squad car at the head of the driveway. Officer Lopez took the driver's seat, Officer Whipple rode shotgun, and the three of us piled into the back.

"Can we decide the radio station?" Bess asked, then snorted. "Just kidding!"

Officer Whipple shot an annoyed look behind

him. "Keep it quiet back there," he warned. "Officially, we don't have any passengers."

Officer Lopez pulled the car onto the Strip and began maneuvering around taxis, shuttle buses, and tourists' cars.

A muffled voice came through the radio. Xavier's car had been spotted at a stoplight a few blocks down.

"Jackpot," Officer Lopez whispered, and began heading that way.

As we approached the Gully Ranch casino with its giant neon cacti circling the driveway, I spotted a modest silver car pulling away from the intersection ahead. "There he is!"

Officer Lopez accelerated, then settled in two cars behind Xavier. "Great. We've got him now."

"The chase is on! Are you going to turn on the lights and siren?" George asked eagerly.

"No," Officer Lopez replied. "There's no need to draw attention to ourselves. If he sees us following him, he'll either surrender or do everything he can to lose us, which might endanger innocent citizens. If we don't make a big show of following, we're hoping he might lead us to Veronica."

I nodded. The officers' reasoning made good sense to me. And I desperately hoped that it was that simple: that Xavier was keeping Veronica somewhere, and we could still find her and save her.

We followed the car along the Strip, then onto a highway. Officer Lopez was a good driver and managed to keep within sight of Xavier, but not close enough for him to notice that we were behind him. It was getting later, and darkness was falling as we drove along several car lengths behind the rented Malibu. I tried to still the anxiety I felt building in my chest. How long would we be following Xavier? Where would he lead us? And what would we find when we got there?

As it turned out, our chase wasn't as dramatic as I was expecting. Xavier pulled off the highway only about fifteen miles south of where he'd gotten on. The vibe was very different here: instead of the bright neon lights and lingering crowds of the Strip, we were on a small, run-down commercial strip in the desert.

We saw only a few other cars on the street and passed two pawnshops, a thrift store, and a liquor store. Then nothing but the empty desert.

We drove about a half mile before a TUMBLEWEED MOTEL sign appeared on the right. A short, narrow driveway flanked an old-looking one-story roadside motel, covered in dirt-colored stucco. There was a small overhang with an OFFICE sign, but Xavier pulled right past it, parking the car in front of the far side of the building.

Officer Lopez hung back for a moment, letting the squad car disappear into the shadows until it was clear Xavier hadn't seen us. "A motel," she breathed. "That could mean . . ."

Just as she spoke, Xavier jumped out of his car and stared at the building. He was squinting and looking around as though he was reading the numbers on a few different rooms. *Does he not know where he's going?* That would be good, right? Unless he'd had his goons do the dirty work for him. As he hesitated, the door on the room farthest from the office burst open.

Xavier let out a cry of surprise as Veronica ran out toward him. She was still wearing her leggings and sweatshirt, and her hair looked dirty and uncombed. She looked exhausted, rumpled, and worse for wear—but she was very much alive!

CHAPTER THIRTEEN

❧

The Bride's Back?

"DON'T MOVE!" OFFICER LOPEZ BARKED AT us. Before Bess, George, or I could even react, she and Officer Whipple had thrown open their doors and jumped out of the car.

"Hands up!" she screamed in Xavier and Veronica's direction. "Police!"

Veronica was facing us, and her mouth dropped open as she stopped short and raised her hands into the air. I could see red marks around her wrists, possibly where they'd been bound. Xavier looked over his shoulder, clearly taken off guard, and put his hands up over his head too.

"Officers!" he cried. "This isn't what it looks like! I can explain!"

"Turn around and put your hands on the car," Officer Whipple yelled back. "You can tell us your story when we're sure you're not armed."

Both Veronica and Xavier leaned on Xavier's rental car, and the officers lowered their guns, ran over, and quickly frisked them. Seemingly finding no weapons, they handcuffed Xavier, then led him and Veronica over to a bench in front of the room Veronica had come out of.

"Wait . . . so he was holding her hostage, but he doesn't have a weapon?" Bess asked, frowning at me.

"I don't know," I said. "Maybe he has one in the car? But this isn't happening like I thought it would."

"Veronica looked pretty happy to see him," George added. "The way she ran at him—I don't think that's how I would approach the guy who abducted me!"

"Unless she doesn't know?" I suggested. "Maybe she's only dealt with his hired help." Then I gasped as another thought occurred to me. Bess and George looked over, and I felt a little guilty as I put my thoughts into words. "Or," I said softly, "maybe they staged her disappearance? For views or money?"

George winced. And Bess shook her head.

"Veronica would *never*," she insisted. "She's too smart for that!"

I nodded. "Yeah, you're probably right."

Bess looked thoughtful. "I guess we'll find out the truth soon. . . ."

The officers were speaking more quietly with Xavier and Veronica. Cautiously, I knocked on the window of the back seat of the cruiser. When Officer Whipple looked over, I shot him a plaintive *Can we get out now?* look. It was going to kill me to watch the police find out what was going on here while we sat in the back of a police car and waited. Officer Whipple looked at Officer Lopez, who glanced at me and nodded curtly. As Officer Lopez faced Xavier and Veronica and holstered her weapon, Officer Whipple came over to the cruiser and opened our door.

"Thanks!" I said brightly. "We just really want to hear what happened."

Officer Whipple didn't crack a smile. "Now that we know the suspect is unarmed and in cuffs, you can listen, but don't get cocky," he warned. "You may be investigating this case, but you're teenagers. We shouldn't have brought you along in the first place, because your parents could sue the pants off us. Don't do anything rash and make us regret it!"

I decided not to tell him that my dad is in fact a very well-known attorney who could sue off not only his pants, but probably his shirt and shoes, too. But Dad is used to looking the other way when I take reasonable risks in my sleuthing. Instead I just smiled and hurried closer to where Officer Lopez was questioning Veronica and Xavier. Nancy Drew and law enforcement: What can I say? Sometimes we get along, and sometimes, not so much. I try not to worry about it. The important thing is that the crooks get caught.

George and Bess were right behind me. And when Veronica spotted us, her face lit up.

"Omigosh, Bess! George! How did you . . . ?"

Officer Lopez turned to give us a wry smile. "These three have taken an active interest in your case," she said simply. "You're very lucky to have friends who care about you so deeply. If not for them, we may not have found you."

"Are you okay?" Bess asked eagerly, reaching a hand out to Veronica. "We've been so, so worried."

Veronica took Bess's hand and squeezed it. "I'm okay," she said, "partly thanks to you and Nancy, I guess."

Officer Lopez looked at Xavier. "Okay. So tell us again how you ended up here."

Xavier looked utterly confused. "I told you. I got a call from an unknown number. When I answered it, it was Veronica."

"And you've never been here before?" Officer Lopez sounded dubious. "Security camera footage will back that up?"

Xavier raised his shoulders. "Dude, I didn't know this place existed! I'm not from Vegas! I got a call from

V, and I was just so relieved to hear her voice! She said they were holding her at the Tumbleweed Motel, and I ran down the Strip, rented a car, and plugged the name into GPS."

Officer Lopez frowned at Veronica. "Why would you call him instead of the police?"

Veronica looked embarrassed, glancing from the officers to Xavier. "I know it doesn't make sense," she admitted. "I just . . . love him so much. When I wanted to feel safe, I thought of him first. And I guess part of me felt really bad for skipping out on our wedding. Especially when I realized he had nothing to do with the guys who were holding me."

"Guys?" Officer Whipple asked. He'd followed us over from the cruiser. "What guys?"

"I don't know," Veronica replied, her eyes wide. "I'd never seen them before the day of our wedding. I was getting ready to leave the casino and take a cab to the airport—I had my passport and a credit card in my sweatshirt pocket—but then the elevator stopped on the third floor at the casino, and they were there, these two big guys. One showed me a gun, and they told me to get out and follow them. They shoved this hat on my head to cover my face, then put me in a van and brought me here. They've been guarding me in the motel room ever since."

"So where *are* they?" Officer Lopez asked, reaching for her gun as she looked nervously at the motel building. "In the room?"

"No." Veronica shook her head. "They leave every so often to get food or, I don't know, meet with whoever they work for. Usually one would go, one would watch me. Today, they tied me to a chair and they both went. I managed to wriggle out, and I called Xavier from the landline in the room."

Officer Whipple's eyes flicked to Xavier. "How can you be sure Xavier *isn't* the one they're working for?"

Xavier gasped. "Bro!"

Veronica sighed. "Because I trust him," she said simply.

Officer Whipple exchanged a glance with Officer Lopez, then pulled out his phone. "Here it is," he said, flipping through his emails. "The station was able to find it." He pulled a document up on his screen and held it out to show Veronica. "Did you know about this, miss?"

Veronica stared at the screen, scrunching up her eyebrows in confusion. "What am I looking at?"

"It's a life insurance policy," Officer Lopez replied, looking from Veronica to Xavier. "Xavier took it out on you four days ago. To the tune of one point five million dollars."

"*What?!*" Xavier shook his head at Officer Lopez, then looked desperately at Veronica. "Babe, I would never. I don't even—"

"Then why is your signature on it?" Officer Whipple demanded. "We know your business was in trouble. You had motive. . . ."

"Are you saying I tried to *hurt* her?" Xavier asked, disbelieving. "For *money?* And what do you even mean about my *business?*"

As Xavier argued with the officers, I looked at Veronica. Notably, she didn't look surprised. She had the sad, resigned expression I remembered from the night before the wedding. *So did she know?* I wondered. *Is that why she left the wedding? But why did she call him for help?* My brain felt like it was whirling around at a hundred miles an hour, trying to absorb all this information.

"Redd Zone owes a quarter of a million dollars," Officer Whipple was saying to Xavier. "If something happened to Veronica, you'd get a massive life insurance payout. Are you trying to tell me there's no connection?"

Xavier shook his head. "I am telling you, Officer," he said, "I didn't do that. I thought Redd Zone was doing fine! And I would *never* hurt Veronica! She's the love of my life!"

Despite everything that was going on, Veronica looked touched by that. "Oh, babe," she said softly.

"And when she called you, you didn't come back in and alert the police?" Officer Lopez put in. "Even though you had a room full of security on hand?"

Xavier sighed. "I know, I know. Maybe it was

stupid of me. But I just heard her voice and I had to *get* here, you know? I was so afraid . . . I was so afraid something had happened to her."

All at once, something clicked in my brain. The whirling stopped.

The police definitely did *not* look touched by Xavier's explanation. "So who did this?" Officer Lopez demanded.

I held up my hand hesitantly. An idea was slowly taking shape. "Uh—I think I might know," I said.

All eyes turned to me.

"Omigosh, spit it out, Nancy," George urged. "Please. Did Xavier do this or not?"

"I think . . ." I cleared my throat. "Not."

"Thank you," Xavier breathed, as Veronica regarded me with wide, dark eyes.

Officer Lopez placed a hand on her hip. "Okay," she said. "Let's do this, then, teen sleuth. Tell me your theory."

"Well," I said, "it would have to be someone who knows Xavier well. Well enough to forge his signature.

And it would have to be someone who knows Redd Zone's finances—and knows what terrible shape they're in."

"I don't get this," Xavier said, shaking his head. "We're doing fine! All the social med—"

He dropped off suddenly as the sound of an engine approached. We all turned to spot another car driving along the street and pulling into the Tumbleweed Motel's driveway.

"Oh!" Bess gasped.

Was this Veronica's captors returning to find her freed?

It was a nondescript white SUV with Nevada plates. *Probably a rental,* I thought. When the driver seemed to spot our group, they stopped the car abruptly just after pulling in and idled near the office. But Officer Whipple pulled a flashlight out from his belt and shone a ridiculously bright light in the direction of the driver's seat. The driver shaded his eyes, cringing.

But we could all see that it was Max.

I was right!

Officer Lopez drew her gun and pointed it at the SUV. "Hands up! Police!"

Slowly, Max put his hands up.

"I knew it!" Veronica suddenly yelled. "Whatever was going on with the store, I knew Xavier loved me too much to hurt me!"

We all turned to look at her. Her eyes were bright as she went on to explain, "I got cold feet when my uncle told me what bad shape Redd Zone was really in . . . and then Xavier had his accident at the rehearsal dinner after we switched suits. Once he switched suits with me, suddenly he got worried about how dark it was and whether the jump was safe, even though he'd been pushing to do it a minute before. It just felt like too much of a coincidence."

"Babe, no!" Xavier cried. "I would *never* hurt you! Ever!"

Veronica glanced at him, tearing up a little. "I know that now. At the hospital, thinking this all over, I thought maybe you'd changed your mind, or you hoped the parachute might deploy anyway. But I wanted time to talk to you about it, alone. I realized that even if it wasn't you, *someone* might be trying to hurt me. That's why I ran away from the wedding. But when I was abducted, I heard one of the men speaking to someone on the phone who sounded like Max. And I realized, he needed money just as badly as Xavier. So I thought I could trust Xavier enough to call him for help. . . ."

"Stop! No!"

Officer Lopez's shout cut the air as the SUV was suddenly thrown into drive and started to screech out of the parking lot.

CHAPTER FOURTEEN

~

Extreme Dysfunction

"COME ON!" OFFICER LOPEZ SHOUTED AT Officer Whipple, and before the rest of us could say anything, they'd bolted back to the police cruiser and squealed out after Max, sirens blaring.

I turned and looked at my friends, Veronica, and Xavier. "Uh . . . I think we just lost our ride."

"No! Seriously?" Bess cried, lifting her hands in frustration. "After all that? We're going to miss the climax?"

Xavier put his head in his hands. "Nooooo," he moaned. "Even though Max betrayed me . . . that's still my brother! What if he does something stupid, like threaten the police?"

Veronica whipped her head toward him. "You think he would do that?"

Xavier nodded, groaning. "I don't know what he's capable of. He's obviously had some kind of mental break, V. And even after all he's done, he's still my little brother, and I would never forgive myself if something happened to him. Do we have to just wait here to find out if he survived the chase?"

I glanced at Bess and George. They looked as nervous as I was feeling. Max had done some terrible things, but he was heading into a dangerous confrontation, and Xavier didn't deserve to lose his brother.

"Not if I have anything to say about it," Veronica announced, jumping to her feet. She looked down at Xavier. "Where are your car keys?"

"In the car," Xavier replied, lifting his own cuffed wrists. "But, uh, slight problem . . ."

"Get up," Veronica commanded, grabbing his elbow and lifting him from the bench. "You're in the back seat. Nancy, I trust you to find Max, so you're riding shotgun. Let's go, there's no time to lose!"

She led Xavier over to his rented Chevy and we all piled in. Veronica jumped into the driver's seat. Bess and George helped Xavier sit down in the back. And I took shotgun. Pretty soon we were screeching out of the parking lot, following in the direction of the police and Max.

Within about thirty seconds, we'd caught up.

"He's going farther into the desert," George observed. "They turned in the opposite direction from the highway."

Veronica nodded grimly. "Makes sense. Max lived in Vegas for a while after college. He probably knows exactly where he's going."

A groan sounded from the back seat. "I just hope he's not planning something stupid," Xavier moaned. "Babe, I can't believe he would do this to you! I had no idea! He never even told me the business was in trouble!"

"I believe you," Veronica said quickly. We were

approaching an intersection. The police cruiser was still about twenty yards ahead of us, and Max's SUV was maybe fifteen yards in front of them. Max sped through the stoplight as it turned from green to yellow. The cruiser just barely made it through before the light turned red.

"Go!" Bess cried. "We can't lose them!"

Veronica had been shifting her foot to hit the brake, but at Bess's words, she stepped heavily back onto the gas, and we barreled into the intersection. Cars on the cross street had just started to accelerate toward the intersection, and they jammed on their horns and abruptly stopped to avoid us.

Veronica hit the gas even harder, speeding to catch up to the cruiser.

"Oh my gosh," she whispered. "I am normally, like, the *most* careful driver."

"But this dude tried to kill you, cuz!" George reminded her.

Veronica nodded, focusing on the road. "That's right," she said. "I want Max to survive, but I still want to see them lead him away in handcuffs!"

We were on a small highway now, two lanes through the desert with a rocky median in between. Our three cars were going faster than any of the other cars, and soon we were alone, three cars following each other through the gathering darkness. The desert landscape blurred on the edges of the road. We went a mile on this highway, then two, then five.

"Where is he *going*?" Bess whined impatiently. "Like, are we going to be in California when this ends?"

"He'll run out of gas before California," George said. "I mean, I hope."

The police seemed to be getting impatient too. Gradually they began drawing closer to the SUV Max was driving, as though trying to goad him into stopping. The lights were on and the siren was going full blast. I could barely hear anything else.

As we approached an exit, the cruiser suddenly advanced to the left of the SUV, and then began gradually shifting to the right.

"What are they doing?" Xavier cried. "They're going to hit him!"

"But they know he doesn't want to be hit," I replied. "They're trying to force him off at the exit. They probably think it will be harder for him to avoid them on a local street."

Sure enough, the white SUV was pulling closer to the exit ramp. Veronica shifted into the right lane to follow.

But then, out of nowhere, Max slammed on the gas, pulling not onto the exit ramp—but off the road entirely, into the desert.

"Are you kidding me!" Veronica shrieked as the SUV maneuvered around some low cacti and a pile of rocks. "He has four-wheel drive, I don't!"

But the cruiser was already pulling off the road to follow.

"I think this would violate the rental agreement," Xavier said solemnly from the back seat.

"Really?" Veronica said.

"Ahhhh, forget it. Apparently, I'm broke anyway!" Xavier said after a moment. "What's one more rental car penalty?"

"All right then!" Veronica pulled off the highway

and carefully steered along after the cruiser. It was lucky that we were third in line and could follow a sort of "path" made by the other two cars through the sand. But it was still pretty freaky. The desert was dark, and it was hard to tell what we were driving over. The car thumped heavily over the uneven surface, and I grabbed the handle over the passenger door to hold on.

"Where is he taking us?" I asked after a few minutes of desert driving. "If he thought he was going to lose us off-roading, he's clearly wrong. So what now?"

Up ahead, we suddenly saw the flashing red of brake lights.

"He's stopping," Veronica said. As the police cruiser slowed down, she did too. Soon all three vehicles were at a stop.

It was nearly completely dark. I had no idea where we were—until I spotted a small wooden sign and a parking lot.

FRICK CANYON PARK.

"Guys!" I hissed. "We're at the park where the rehearsal dinner took place!"

Bess and George looked around.

"Oh gosh, you're right!" George said. "That's where the taco truck was, and—"

"Omigosh." Veronica suddenly looked stricken. There was action up ahead, and as a door opened on the SUV, she threw the car into park, unclipped her seat belt, and vaulted out the door.

"Don't forget me!" Xavier cried.

Abruptly, Veronica stopped, ran back, and opened the back door, then reached down to help Xavier to his feet. He was still handcuffed, making it hard to maneuver on his own.

I threw open my own door and jumped out. I could just make out a figure running out of the SUV . . . and toward the steep cliff Xavier and Veronica had BASE jumped off.

That jump had nearly killed Xavier. That jump was far too steep for anyone to survive with no protective equipment.

My heart beat faster. Could Max be that desperate?

I fell into step behind Veronica, my feet thudding

along the sand as I raced to the edge of the cliff.

Officers Lopez and Whipple were just ahead of us. As we ran, Officer Whipple spun around and aimed his flashlight at us. *"What are you doing here?"* he demanded, sounding furious.

"We wanted to make sure Max didn't do anything rash," I yelled. "We hoped he would listen to his big brother!"

Officer Whipple swung his flashlight toward Max again, illuminating a very strange scene.

Max was standing with his back to the cliff, frantically . . . getting dressed? Yes, I realized as I drew closer. Max was pulling on a bright white wingsuit, similar to the ones Xavier and Veronica had worn for their jump after the rehearsal dinner.

He shoved his arm into the last sleeve and yanked the collar to his neck.

What is he planning?!

Officer Lopez already had her gun trained on him. "Don't do this, Max," she warned in a low voice.

"Xavier," Max said, ignoring the officer. His voice

was strained and weary sounding. "I have something I need to tell you."

Xavier moved forward. He was bringing up the rear of our little procession, led by Veronica. "Uh, yeah, bro," he said, shaking his head and lifting his cuffed wrists. "I'd say you have *a few* things you need to tell me."

But Max went on as though he hadn't heard. "Xavier, the Redd Zone is in major debt," he said. "I'm sorry. I should have told you earlier. But we're about to lose everything. We're about to be bankrupt, man. I've made a lot of bad decisions."

Xavier drew to a stop in front of me, staring at his brother. "I would say so," he said. "But please, man, don't do anything you'll regret. Whatever happened, you're still my brother."

Max drew up to his full height, looking almost proud of himself as he looked straight at Xavier. "I had this idea. An idea I thought could get us out of trouble . . ."

"I know what your idea was," Xavier said, shaking

his head disbelievingly. "*Kill Veronica?* I can't believe that thought even entered your mind! What did you think would happen to me? You know how much I love her."

Max shrugged. "I do," he said. "But . . . I guess I thought you'd get over it! Eventually, I mean. You take crazy risks all the time! You thrive on them! So I tried to make it look like an accident, so you would never know."

Veronica let out a snort of disgust.

"You disabled her parachute at the rehearsal dinner," I accused him, remembering how Max had been in charge of the "safety precautions" for all the extreme-sports stunts. "You thought she would die during the jump, and it would look like a tragic accident. But you didn't anticipate her switching suits with Xavier."

Max glanced over at me, nodding. "Oh," he said. "Nancy. Hello. Yes, you're right about that," he agreed.

"I don't believe this," Veronica scoffed.

"So I made another plan," Max continued. "I was going to bungle Veronica's BASE jump off the roof-deck of the Soar. Xavier was unable to jump because of his injuries, but Veronica still would have done it, especially once I explained to her how important it was to show our followers on social media that we believe in the extreme-sports lifestyle. But then Veronica disappeared." He frowned, turning to Veronica with a glare. "I suspected it when she headed off without her bridesmaids. I could only assume she got cold feet—maybe she'd gotten wind of my plan! And all I could see was our only chance to save the business running away."

"A *'chance to save the business'*?" Veronica asked in disgust. "That's what you saw?"

Xavier lifted his cuffed hands to his face, covering his eyes. "I don't believe this, dude."

Max sighed. "I had hired some local tough guys," he said, "and they were waiting on standby, in case I had to make a speedy getaway. So when Veronica excused herself, supposedly to fix her veil, I texted them some quick instructions: instead of helping me escape, use the van to abduct Veronica."

That was one thing I didn't understand. "How did you find her?" I asked.

"Well," Max said, turning to me with a pleased expression, "I knew she would need to come down in the elevator, of course. So I gave my men a description and had them wait on the restaurant floor, pressing the button and checking every elevator until they found her. Fortunately, her disguise was not that hard to see through."

Bess let out a sigh. "What happened then?" she asked.

"Yeah, Veronica is still alive," George pointed out. "And I thought your plan was to kill her. That's what you saw running away, right? Your chance to kill her and make it look like an accident, bailing you out from all your terrible business decisions."

Veronica nodded. "Right. What happened to your *brilliant* plan?"

Max glanced at her, then looked at Xavier, his eyes wide. "The only problem was," he said, "when I saw how upset Xavier was about losing Veronica . . . I couldn't do it." He shook his head. "It was one thing to mess with the safety equipment, but I was quickly learning, I am not the type of person who could murder someone in cold blood—or even ask someone else to do it. I've been fighting my conscience since then. I asked my men to hold her in the motel. And just today, in fact, I had decided to set her free. . . ."

Veronica let out a sharp laugh. "Sure you did."

Max looked at her blankly. "But Xavier beat me to it," he finished. "You reached him, and he came to rescue you. How romantic!"

Xavier let out a cold chuckle. "Romantic! Max, you don't know what real love is. You love me, but you thought you could kill Veronica and we would just . . . *be okay?*"

Max looked sheepish. "You were never supposed to know. If things had gone as planned, you would have thought you lost your wife in a tragic accident."

Xavier shook his head. "I can't believe you."

Max dropped his gaze to the ground. "I'm sorry. Our financial situation was getting worse and worse, and I was desperate. I didn't want to lose everything we'd worked so hard for."

"Why wouldn't you tell me the business was in trouble?" Xavier demanded. "Especially when it was *this* bad?"

Max sighed, looking up at Xavier. "At first I didn't want to worry you. I thought we could save it. You could always sell ice to a snowman, Xavier. I thought, if we just pushed really hard, used our social media following, *acted* like we were a success—"

"But dude," Xavier cut in. "A quarter of a million? How could we ever dig out of that?"

Max shook his head again. "I think I didn't want to admit that we couldn't, even to myself. I had failed in my job. And I always looked up to you, Xavier. When we were little, you talked about starting a business with Arlo. When you asked me to go in with you instead, I was shocked— and I wanted so badly to show you I was the right choice."

Veronica stared at him. "By killing his wife," she said. "Wow. Is that what they teach you in business school?"

Max turned to her. "Veronica, I—"

Veronica lifted her hand. "Save it," she said. "Call me irrational, but there is literally nothing you can say to me right now that would make me okay with your trying to kill me, Max. I mean, I guess it's nice you changed your mind? But I don't think we'll be sharing any Thanksgiving dinners."

"I just want to—" Max tried to go on, but Veronica shook her head.

"Rot in prison, you sociopath," she said, then turned on her heel and began to walk away.

Max looked back at the ground.

"I think it's time to come with us, Max," Officer Whipple said. "Hands up. Let's make this nice and easy."

Max looked up at the officers, almost beseechingly.

But then . . . he started to laugh.

"Oh, great," Officer Lopez muttered. "I knew it. He's one of those mustache-twirling types."

"The thing is," Max said between giggles, "I can't go to prison. I don't have the constitution for it. That's what this wingsuit is for. I've been carrying it in my rental car, just in case I needed to escape. I'll be on my way now . . . en route, I called my colleagues to meet me with a car across the valley. From there we'll head to Mexico."

He gestured to the far distance.

"Are you out of your mind?!" Xavier shouted. "*I'm the daredevil, and I couldn't make it that far. You've never even done this before!*"

Max looked at him for a moment, then shrugged sadly. "I find myself with very few options. Goodbye, Xavier."

He lifted his arms in the air, opening the "wings" on the wingsuit. My heart was pounding in my throat. *Don't do it!* Max was clearly a few tacos short of a combo platter, but this was his worst plan yet. He would surely die in the attempt. I thought Veronica was right about a lot of things: Max didn't deserve our pity. He deserved punishment. But he didn't deserve to die in a crumpled heap at the bottom of a desert canyon. I knew Xavier would never forgive himself for letting it happen.

He lifted one foot over the edge of the cliff. . . .

"*Stop!*" I screamed, an idea suddenly occurring to me. "That's the suit with the disabled parachute, the one you tried to give Veronica! *Don't jump! You'll die!*"

Max abruptly stopped and moved his head just slightly to turn back over his shoulder. For a few seconds, he stood there, no doubt debating whether what I'd claimed was possible. I had no idea whether it was or not. All I needed was a moment of hesitation.

And that was all it took. In that second, Officers Lopez and Whipple darted forward, tackling Max to the ground just inches away from a drop steep enough to kill all of them.

I hadn't realized I'd stopped breathing, but when I started again, it felt amazing. Relief flooded through my body as the officers handcuffed Max and brought him back to his feet. I turned to my friends, thrilled that we'd just barely averted a tragedy. And Xavier *wasn't* a bad guy! And he and Veronica might work it out!

"I knew you'd save the day, Nancy!" Bess moved

over and hugged me, and George followed, piling onto her hug.

"Nice thinking there, Sherlock," George agreed. "That's why I hang out with you."

When they pulled back, Xavier and Veronica were waiting. Xavier was still handcuffed while the police dealt with Max, but they both looked relieved.

"I can't thank you enough," Xavier said, "even if you did think I was a murderer there for a minute."

I winced. "I mean, I still think my reasoning was sound?"

Veronica swatted at him. "It was! Seriously, *thank you*, Nancy. Thank you for getting the police here, for saving the day . . . and for very likely saving Max's life."

"Oh, it's no problem," I said, watching the officers lead a cuffed Max over to the police cruiser. "It's kind of . . . what I'm here for."

CHAPTER FIFTEEN

~❦~

Another Chance

"AND DO YOU, VERONICA ELENA VASQUEZ, take Xavier Leroy Redd as your lawfully wedded husband, to have and to hold, to love and to cherish . . ."

Bess reached over and squeezed my arm. I looked over at her, and she shot me one of her patented, *Can you believe this? This is so romantic I'm about to burst!* looks. She even waved her hands over her head, mimicking an explosion: *mind blown*. I winked at her and nodded. Yup, it was finally happening. Three months after their failed wedding attempt (and Max's failed murder attempt) in Las Vegas, Xavier and Veronica were finally having a public wedding ceremony at a beautiful flower farm outside Chicago. It was a smaller ceremony—no attendants, even fewer guests, no extreme sports. Notably, though, Veronica and Deanna's parents were in attendance this time. I guess any romance that could survive a murder attempt was strong enough to convince even the most protective mom and dad. And to look at Xavier's and Veronica's faces, all the love from that failed ceremony was still there—plus a little more, now that they knew how much they could truly trust each other.

" . . . until death do you part?" the officiant finished.

Veronica startled slightly, then found Xavier's eyes. I would bet they were both thinking about how close Veronica had come to death already as a result of this marriage, but thankfully, the danger was over now. Max was still in Nevada, in jail awaiting trial for attempted murder, along with a host of other charges. Unfortunately for Max and his constitution, it looked like he was headed for prison for a long time.

"I do," Veronica said, and both she and Xavier beamed.

"Then by the power vested in me by the state of Illinois, I now pronounce you husband and wife. You may now kiss!"

Veronica leaned in hungrily, and both she and Xavier laughed as they smooched. I glanced to my other side at Ned, who nudged me with a smile and then pulled a handkerchief out of his pocket and handed it to me. Was I crying? Oh no—I'd teared up. I used the handkerchief to wipe my eyes as the crowd began whooping at the bride and groom.

"You're not usually this sentimental, Nancy," Ned leaned down to whisper. "Are you picturing your own wedding?"

I chuckled, but not unkindly. Ned smiled. He knows I'm crazy about him, but I'm not really the fantasizing-about-my-wedding type. Still, it was nice to be attending this new celebration with a plus-one.

The music swelled, and everyone cheered as the bride and groom strode down the aisle together for the first time as husband and wife. When I looked at Bess and George, they were dabbing away tears too.

"It all worked out for them," George observed, shaking her head. "I almost can't believe it! Those two crazy kids really want to be married."

"Of course they do, George," Bess said, shoving her tissue back into her tiny purse. "It's true love!"

As the bride and groom and their immediate families (minus those in jail) headed off to take pictures, I wandered with Ned, Bess, and George to the cocktail hour, which was taking place on a little deck a few yards from the ceremony spot. Ned grabbed us all some sparkling cider, and we settled down on some benches to chat.

"Just think, Nancy," Bess said, "if it wasn't for Xavier and Veronica, you never would have tried flyboarding."

I gave her a wry grin. "If it wasn't for Xavier and Veronica, I wouldn't have done a lot of things."

"You really seemed to enjoy flyboarding, though," Ned suggested, leaning back and wrapping his arm around my shoulders. "I mean, going by the video you texted me. In fact, I found a link to it on Instagram. Did you know you're famous?"

I groaned. "Am I still online? Are all the Redd Zone social media sites still up?" Sadly, the complex had closed this month, after a massive going-out-of-business sale. Veronica and Xavier still did a little thrill seeking on their own, but the Redd Zone was no more. Xavier was filing for bankruptcy, but he and Veronica were working with her uncle to try to come up with a financial recovery plan. Already, I'd heard, Arlo had reached out to Xavier with a proposal for a *new* business—this one, an employment training and placement firm that would help recently released prisoners get back on their feet. Bess said Xavier was really interested. It turned out he and Arlo *did* have a special friendship—the kind that can go quiet for years, but then they were able to pick up right where they'd left off.

Speaking of friends, I spotted Priya and Deanna at a table together with their husbands. Deanna was telling a story and Priya was laughing hysterically. I nudged Bess and George. "I guess those two worked out their differences, huh?"

Bess followed my glance and nodded. "Oh yeah. Well, it helps that they were both *sort of* right—Veronica really was in danger, but not from Xavier, who really is a stand-up guy."

"I always thought Priya and Deanna would get along if they could just get past the Xavier stuff," George said. "They have a lot in common."

"Yeah, for one, they're both super dedicated to Veronica," I agreed. It was nice to see Priya and Deanna having a good time after worrying so much about their sister and friend. For once, all was well that ended well—it was a beautiful day, we were home with our friends, and we'd just watched two very happy people promise to share their lives. I let out a little sigh and leaned back against Ned.

Bess glanced at me out of the corner of her eye. "You know," she said, "I think we all learned that it's good to push yourself out of your comfort zone sometimes."

"Did we?" George asked skeptically. "Is that what we learned? Because it kinda looked that way in the beginning, but . . ."

Bess waved her away and went on. "Like, for example, Nancy and I had these *amazing* experiences bungee jumping and flyboarding. We never could have done that if we hadn't pushed out of our little boxes. Right, Nancy?"

Why did this sound familiar? "Bess, what are you getting at?"

Bess grinned and leaned toward me eagerly. "Well! I was on Instagram the other day, looking around at some other extreme-sports accounts. And I found this extreme-sports club that meets up in Chicago. It's for all ages, and they're going on a bungee-jumping trip next weekend! I'm seriously thinking about it. And I just thought, you had a nice time flyboarding, and maybe *George* would be open to trying something new. . . ."

"*No,*" George said curtly. "That's a hard no, if you're wondering. No offense. But that stuff is *not* for me, especially after we saw Xavier almost die in that canyon. . . ."

Bess shrugged and looked at me hopefully. "And you, Nancy?"

I could feel Ned watching me curiously. And I knew the Nancy he'd fallen for would easily say no. But the thing is, I *had* learned something from Xavier that weekend in Vegas. No matter how crazy an idea might seem, I didn't want to live my life in a box. I wanted to reserve the right to consider everything.

I glanced at Ned, then raised my glass toward Bess. "Well," I said, "never say never."

Dear Diary,

SEE? I WAS RIGHT TO BE WORRIED! But even in my most anxious moments, I couldn't have predicted Veronica's disappearance, or (briefly) being convinced that her new husband was out to hurt her. I'm glad I was wrong, and that Veronica and Xavier's love was real! I hope they have a wonderful life together now—and that the only thrills they face are the extreme-sports kind.

As for me, I think I've learned to be more open to new experiences. I won't be signing up to heli-ski anytime soon—I get enough goosebumps solving cases!—but I'd like to think I'm more willing to try things. Flyboarding was pretty great! And I'm too young to rule things out completely.

Who knows what's in store for Future Nancy Drew?

New mystery. New suspense. New danger.

Nancy Drew
DIARIES™

BY CAROLYN KEENE

EBOOK EDITIONS AVAILABLE

Aladdin | simonandschuster.com/kids